U0084477

再版序

「中級英語聽力檢定①」是為要參加「全民英語能力檢定測驗」的讀者而設計。用過這本書的讀者，反應這本書，對考試很有用。許多高中採用本書，都認為這本書很好，只是第四部份較難。事實上，「中級英語檢定測驗」的聽力測驗部分，並不考第四部份，第四部份是專為「大學入學推薦甄選第二階段聽力測驗」而設計。參加「中級英語檢定測驗」的讀者，也應該藉此訓練自己的聽力，出乎其上，必得其中。

參加「大學入學推薦甄選第二階段聽力測驗」的考生，只要熟讀本公司出版的「中級英語聽力檢定①」和「中級英語聽力檢定②」，就一定可以高分通過，本書和實際題目大同小異。考試的時候，要先看選項，再聽題目，萬一有一題沒聽懂，要趕快放棄，先看下一題，要超前看選項，不能落後。

本書共分為八回，每回考試時間為 40 分鐘，每回測驗分為四部份，前三部份和教育部的「中級英語檢定測驗」相同。這八回測驗，每回都經過「劉毅英文家教班」同學實際考試，效果良好。每回測驗，每題以 1.67 分計算，最高分介於 79 分至 86 分之間，最低分介於 35 至 42 分之間。每份考題能考 60 分以上，就算及格。

編輯好書是「學習」一貫的宗旨。本書在編審及校對的每一階段，均力求完善，但恐有疏漏之處，誠盼各界先進，不吝批評指正。

編者　謹識

本書製作過程

Test Book No. 1, 4, 7 由蔡琇瑩老師負責，Test Book No. 2, 5, 8 由高瑋謙老師負責，No. 3, 6 由謝靜芳老師負責。每份試題均由三位老師，在聽力班實際測驗過，經過每週一次測驗後，立刻講解的方式，學生們的聽力有明顯的進步，在大學甄試聽力考試中，都輕鬆過關。三位老師們的共同看法是，要在聽力方面得高分，就要不斷練習，愈多愈好。聽力訓練，愈早開始愈好。

本書另附有教學專用本，售價 120 元。

錄音帶八卷，售價 960 元。

English Listening Comprehension Test
Test Book No. 1

This listening comprehension test will test your ability to understand spoken English. In this test, each conversation, statement and question will be spoken JUST ONE TIME. They will not be written out for you. There are four parts to this test. Special instructions will be given to you at the beginning of each part.

Part A

In Part A, you will see several pictures in your test book. For each picture, you will be asked 1 to 3 questions. For each question, you will hear four possible answers. Choose the best answer according to what you see in the picture.

Example:

You will see:

You will hear: What is this?
A. This is a table.
B. This is a chair.
C. This is a watch.
D. This is a doll.

The best answer to the question "What is this?" is B: "This is a chair." Therefore, you should choose answer B.

A. <u>Questions 1-2</u>

C. <u>Questions 5-6</u>

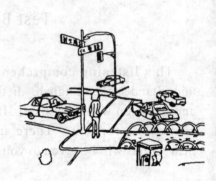

B. <u>Questions 3-4</u>

D. <u>Questions 7-8</u>

E. Questions 9-10

G. Question 13

F. Questions 11-12

H. Questions 14-15

Part B

In Part B, you will hear 15 questions. After you hear a question, read the four possible answers in your test book and decide which one is the best answer to the question you have heard.

Example:

You will hear:　　What does your father do?

You will read:　　A. He's 50 years old.
　　　　　　　　　B. He's a teacher.
　　　　　　　　　C. He's hungry.
　　　　　　　　　D. He's in Los Angeles.

The best answer to the question "What does your father do?" is B: "He's a teacher." Therefore, you should choose answer B.

Please go to the next page. ⇨

16. A. Yes, it's yours.
    B. No, it's not his.
    C. No, it's mine.
    D. No, it's yours.

17. A. You are welcome.
    B. No, thanks.
    C. No, I didn't help you.
    D. How about you?

18. A. Is it real?
    B. I am sorry to hear that.
    C. I don't hear that.
    D. I don't know your father.

19. A. It is a good class.
    B. I like that class.
    C. There are fifty students in that class.
    D. It starts at eight-thirty.

20. A. No, I have one brother.
    B. Yes, I have one sister.
    C. No, I have.
    D. Yes, I have one.

21. A. It's Peter's.
    B. He is an American boy.
    C. It's me, Bill.
    D. Oh, are you my neighbor?

22. A. Sure. You're right.
    B. How did you do it?
    C. Can you do that?
    D. Cheer up! Work harder next time.

23. A. No, they are not interested.
    B. No, it is boring.
    C. Yes, it is interested.
    D. Yes, it is boring.

24. A. Yes, I can give you both hands.
    B. I'm sorry. I'm busy now.
    C. That's a good idea.
    D. No, I can't lend my hand.

25. A. Are you Helen?
    B. Is that Helen?
    C. That's not Helen.
    D. This is Helen.

26. A. It's very hot today.
    B. It's a fine day.
    C. It's March 10.
    D. It's Friday.

27. A. Here are they.
    B. Here they are.
    C. Here it is.
    D. Here are you.

28. A. He likes art.
    B. He's from Keelung.
    C. He gets up at six.
    D. He is a teacher.

29. A. The weekend was too
       short.
    B. That's all right.
    C. We had a good time.
    D. I liked it.

30. A. It won't bite.
    B. It is bigger.
    C. It is broken.
    D. It is expensive.

Part C

In Part C, you will hear 15 conversations between a man and a woman. After each conversation, you will hear a question about the conversation. After you hear the question, read the four possible answers in your test book and choose the best answer to the question you have heard.

Example:

You will hear:　(Man)　　　How do you go to school every day?

　　　　　　　　(Woman)　　Usually by bus.　Sometimes by taxi.

　　　　　　　　TONE:　　　How does the woman go to school?

You will read:　A. She always goes to school on foot.

　　　　　　　　B. She usually takes a bike.

　　　　　　　　C. She takes either a bus or a taxi.

　　　　　　　　D. She usually goes to school by bus, never by taxi.

The best answer to the question "How does the woman go to school?" is C: "She takes either a bus or a taxi."　Therefore, you should choose answer C.

Please go to the next page. ⇨

31. A. It will depend on the
   weather.
   B. He has a better idea.
   C. He wants to be invited.
   D. That's a lot to fit into one
   day.

32. A. A new medicine for
   headaches.
   B. A class they're taking.
   C. The man's job.
   D. The man's health.

33. A. Laura really needs a full-
   time job.
   B. Laura already has a job
   working for the school.
   C. Laura needs to spend her
   time studying.
   D. Laura should think about
   becoming a teacher.

34. A. Look for another seat.
   B. Repeat the question.
   C. Remain standing.
   D. Sit down.

35. A. Put sugar in the tea.
   B. Excuse him.
   C. Repeat what she said.
   D. Allow him to pass.

36. A. Professor Janson has won
   a million dollars.
   B. Professor Janson is lucky
   to be teaching at that
   school.
   C. Teachers like Professor
   Janson are rare.
   D. There are a great many
   teachers of Professor
   Janson's subject.

37. A. She's always running.
   B. She's still in the race.
   C. She feels very comfortable.
   D. She still has a fever.

38. A. How much time the job
   will take.
   B. How the man's health is.
   C. What the man is going
   to do.
   D. If the weather is good today.

39. A. He likes to keep his car looking beautiful.
    B. He wonders who their next neighbor will be.
    C. He admires the neighbor's car.
    D. He hasn't met the new neighbor yet.

40. A. He needs to sleep for three or four hours.
    B. He wants to buy a set of coffee cups.
    C. He will need more than one cup of coffee.
    D. He has been wide awake for some time.

41. A. She wants to borrow his dictionary.
    B. She doesn't know which word he means.
    C. He shouldn't use such big words.
    D. He should look the word up in a dictionary.

42. A. He gets nervous when he goes to dinner parties.
    B. He eats when he needs to calm down.
    C. He thinks the other sandwich would be much better.
    D. He wants the woman to eat the rest of the food.

43. A. Marge has gone home.
    B. Marge feels at home there.
    C. He's known Marge for a long time.
    D. He just met Marge.

44. A. Shelley knows someone there.
    B. Shelley didn't tell him.
    C. He doesn't know who Shelley is.
    D. He wonders which way Shelley went.

45. A. There will be a lot of rain.
    B. Rain is very unlikely.
    C. It's already raining.
    D. She's not sure.

Part D

In Part D, you will hear 15 short talks. After each talk, you will hear a question about the talk. After you hear the question, read the four possible answers in your test book and choose the best answer to the question you have heard.

Example:

You will hear: Well, that's all for Unit 15. For today's
homework, please do the review questions on
page 80, and we'll check the answers tomorrow.
Now, let's go on to Unit 16.

TONE: What is the teacher going to do next in
today's class?

You will read: A. Check the homework.
B. Review Unit 15.
C. Start a new unit.
D. Answer students' questions.

The best answer to the question "What is the teacher going to do next in today's class?" is C: "Start a new unit." Therefore, you should choose answer C.

Please go to the next page. ⇨

46. A. He ate spoiled food.
    B. He ate uncooked food.
    C. He didn't cook food long
       enough.
    D. He ate food just gotten out
       of the oven.

47. A. Children's play balloons.
    B. Weather balloons.
    C. Balloons used for safety
       patrols.
    D. Balloons used for
       recreation.

48. A. Because she'd been born
       that way.
    B. Because a horse had
       kicked her.
    C. Because she'd had a very
       high fever.
    D. Because she'd had a bad
       fall.

49. A. Fifty yards.
    B. Fifty laps.
    C. Once around the yard.
    D. One length of the pool.

50. A. Because he felt strongly
       about slavery.
    B. Because he was defeated
       by Lincoln for president.
    C. Because he was short in
       stature but strong in
       frame.
    D. Because his head was
       larger than his shoulders.

51. A. On the first day of class.
    B. At the end of the first
       week of classes.
    C. Halfway through the
       semester.
    D. Just before the final exam.

52. A. Russian.
    B. German.
    C. French.
    D. Polish.

53. A. Cool.
    B. Warm.
    C. Cloudy.
    D. Sunny.

54. A. The editor.
    B. A journalism professor.
    C. The budget director.
    D. An engineer.

55. A. Commercial fishing.
    B. Biology.
    C. Mechanical engineering.
    D. Computer programming.

56. A. Bicycles and cars.
    B. Building codes.
    C. Energy conservation.
    D. New housing construction.

57. A. The life of Emily Dickinson.
    B. The poetry of Walt Whitman.
    C. The work of Professor May.
    D. The life of Walt Whitman.

58. A. Students.
    B. Government officials.
    C. City planners.
    D. Fishermen.

59. A. After class.
    B. At the beginning of the term.
    C. In the fall.
    D. Before vacation.

60. A. 1588.
    B. 1603.
    C. 1683.
    D. 1688.

Listening Test 1 詳解

Part A

For questions number 1 to 2, please look at picture A.

1. (**B**) Question number 1, where is the teacher standing?
    A. She is standing on the chair.
    B. She is standing on the platform.
    C. She is standing on the desk.
    D. She is standing on the book shelf.
    * platform (ˈplætˌfɔrm) *n.* 講台

2. (**C**) Question number 2, please look at picture A again. What is the subject that she is teaching?
    A. She is teaching English.
    B. She is teaching chemistry.
    C. She is teaching geography.
    D. She is teaching physics.

For questions number 3 to 4, please look at picture B.

3. (**C**) Question number 3, how many people work in this office?
    A. There are five people working in this office.
    B. There are six people working in this office.
    C. There are four people working in this office.
    D. There are three people working in this office.

4. (**A**) Question number 4, please look at picture B again. What is the man sitting on the upper left doing?
    A. He is typing.
    B. He is answering the telephone.
    C. He is using an adding machine.
    D. He is using the fax machine.

For questions number 5 to 6, please look at picture C.

5. (**B**) Question number 5, what is this a typical picture of?
　　　A. This is a typical picture of a rest room.
　　　B. This is a typical picture of an intersection.
　　　C. This is a typical picture of an airport.
　　　D. This is a typical picture of a supermarket.

　　　* intersection (ˌɪntə'sɛkʃən) *n.* 十字路口

6. (**C**) Question number 6, please look at picture C again.　What is the man doing on the safety island?
　　　A. He is talking over a telephone.
　　　B. He is walking across the street.
　　　C. He is waiting to cross the street.
　　　D. He is working for the gas station.

　　　* *safety island* 安全島

For questions number 7 to 8, please look at picture D.

7. (**A**) Question number 7, what is on fire?
　　　A. A building.
　　　B. A motorcycle.
　　　C. A frost.
　　　D. A book.

　　　* frost (frɔst) *n.* 霜

8. (**A**) Question number 8, please look at picture D again.　What do the firemen wear over their faces?
　　　A. They are wearing helmets and smoke masks.
　　　B. They are wearing blue jeans.
　　　C. They are wearing uniforms.
　　　D. They are wearing beautiful hats.

　　　* helmet ('hɛlmɪt) *n.* 頭盔
　　　uniform ('junə,fɔrm) *n.* 制服

For questions number 9 to 10, please look at picture E.

9. (**A**)　Question number 9, what is the little boy sitting on?
　　　A. The little boy is sitting on a piece of baggage.
　　　B. The little boy is sitting on the floor.
　　　C. The little boy is sitting on the stairs.
　　　D. The little boy is sitting on a chair.

10. (**D**)　Question number 10, please look at picture E again.　Who is coming to help the little boy?
　　　A. A passenger is coming to help him.
　　　B. A waiter is coming to help him.
　　　C. A little girl is coming to help him.
　　　D. A policeman is coming to help him.

For questions number 11 to 12, please look at picture F.

11. (**B**)　Question number 11, why is there a traffic jam?
　　　A. Because a street cleaner is cleaning the streets.
　　　B. Because a car with a flat tire is stopped in the middle of the intersection.
　　　C. Because the traffic lights are out of order.
　　　D. Because there are too many jaywalkers.

　　　* *a flat tire* 爆胎　　*out of order* 故障
　　　jaywalker ('dʒe,wɔkɚ) *n.* 任意穿越馬路的人

12. (**D**)　Question number 12, please look at picture F again.　What are these two policemen doing?
　　　A. They are chasing some criminals.
　　　B. They are crossing the street.
　　　C. They are riding bicycles.
　　　D. One is helping the young man; the other is directing the traffic.

　　　* chase (tʃez) *v.* 追捕　　criminal ('krɪmənḷ) *n.* 罪犯
　　　direct (də'rɛkt) *v.* 指揮

For question number 13, please look at picture G.

13. (**B**) Question number 13, where are the animals?
　　　A. They are at a circus.
　　　B. They are on a farm.
　　　C. They are in a cage.
　　　D. They are in the zoo.

　　* circus ('sɜkəs) *n.* 馬戲團

For questions number 14 to 15, please look at picture H.

14. (**C**) Question number 14, what is the family in the picture doing?
　　　A. They are swimming.
　　　B. They are watching TV.
　　　C. They are having a picnic.
　　　D. They are playing volleyball.

　　* volleyball ('vɑlɪ,bɔl) *n.* 排球

15. (**A**) Question number 15, please look at picture H again.　What are
　　　the boy and the girl throwing?
　　　A. They are throwing a frisbee.
　　　B. They are throwing flippers.
　　　C. They are throwing sunglasses.
　　　D. They are throwing deck chairs.

　　* frisbee ('frɪsbɪ) *n.* 飛盤　　flippers ('flɪpəz) *n.* (海豹等的) 鰭足
　　　deck chair 可摺疊的帆布睡椅

Part B

16. (**D**) Isn't that your car?
　　　A. Yes, it's yours.
　　　B. No, it's not his.
　　　C. No, it's mine.
　　　D. No, it's yours.

17. (**A**) Thank you for your help.
   A. You are welcome.
   B. No, thanks.
   C. No, I didn't help you.
   D. How about you?

18. (**B**) My father has been sick for three weeks.
   A. Is it real?
   B. I am sorry to hear that.
   C. I don't hear that.
   D. I don't know your father.

19. (**D**) What time is your first class?
   A. It is a good class.
   B. I like that class.
   C. There are fifty students in that class.
   D. It starts at eight-thirty.

20. (**D**) Do you have any brothers?
   A. No, I have one brother.
   B. Yes, I have one sister.
   C. No, I have.
   D. Yes, I have one.

21. (**C**) Who is it?
   A. It's Peter's.
   B. He is an American boy.
   C. It's me, Bill.
   D. Oh, are you my neighbor?

22. (**D**) I didn't do well in the English test.
   A. Sure. You're right.
   B. How did you do it?
   C. Can you do that?
   D. Cheer up! Work harder next time.
   * *Cheer up*! 振作點！

23. (**B**) Do you like the movie?
　　　　A. No, they are not interested.
　　　　B. No, it is boring.
　　　　C. Yes, it is interested.
　　　　D. Yes, it is boring.

24. (**B**) Would you please give me a hand?
　　　　A. Yes, I can give you both hands.
　　　　B. I'm sorry.　I'm busy now.
　　　　C. That's a good idea.
　　　　D. No, I can't lend my hand.

25. (**D**) Hello, may I speak to Helen?
　　　　A. Are you Helen?
　　　　B. Is that Helen?
　　　　C. That's not Helen.
　　　　D. This is Helen.

26. (**D**) What day is today?
　　　　A. It's very hot today.
　　　　B. It's a fine day.
　　　　C. It's March 10.
　　　　D. It's Friday.

27. (**B**) I want a sweater and a jacket.
　　　　A. Here are they.
　　　　B. Here they are.
　　　　C. Here it is.
　　　　D. Here are you.

28. (**B**) Where does your father come from?
　　　　A. He likes art.
　　　　B. He's from Keelung.
　　　　C. He gets up at six.
　　　　D. He is a teacher.

29. (**C**) How was your weekend?
    A. The weekend was too short.
    B. That's all right.
    C. We had a good time.
    D. I liked it.

30. (**C**) What's wrong with your watch?
    A. It won't bite.
    B. It is bigger.
    C. It is broken.
    D. It is expensive.

Part C

31. (**A**) W: We can all go swimming at the park after the game.
    M: If it's a nice day, of course!

    (TONE)
    Q: What does the man mean?
    A. It will depend on the weather.
    B. He has a better idea.
    C. He wants to be invited.
    D. That's a lot to fit into one day.
    * *fit into* 適合

32. (**D**) M: I have a headache and a sore throat.
    W: The flu is going around. Do you have a fever or nausea too?

    (TONE)
    Q: What are the man and woman discussing?
    A. A new medicine for headaches.
    B. A class they're taking.
    C. The man's job.
    D. The man's health.
    * *sore throat* 喉嚨痛   flu (flu) *n.* 流行性感冒 (= influenza (ˌɪnfluˈɛnzə))
    go around 流行   nausea (ˈnɔzɪə) *n.* 噁心；想吐

33. (**C**) M: Laura's getting a part-time job next week.
　　　　　 W: Shouldn't she concentrate on doing her school work
　　　　　　　 instead?

　　　　　 (TONE)
　　　　　 Q: What does the woman suggest?

　　　　　 A. Laura really needs a full-time job.
　　　　　 B. Laura already has a job working for the school.
　　　　　 C. Laura needs to spend her time studying.
　　　　　 D. Laura should think about becoming a teacher.

34. (**D**) W: Would you mind if I sat here?
　　　　　 M: Of course not.

　　　　　 (TONE)
　　　　　 Q: What will the woman probably do?

　　　　　 A. Look for another seat.
　　　　　 B. Repeat the question.
　　　　　 C. Remain standing.
　　　　　 D. Sit down.

35. (**C**) W: Please pass me the sugar.
　　　　　 M: Pardon me?

　　　　　 (TONE)
　　　　　 Q: What does the man want the woman to do?

　　　　　 A. Put sugar in the tea.
　　　　　 B. Excuse him.
　　　　　 C. Repeat what she said.
　　　　　 D. Allow him to pass.

　　　　 * *Pardon me*? 對不起，請再說一次好嗎？

36. (**C**) W: This school is lucky to have a teacher as good as Professor Janson.

M: She's one in a million.

(TONE)

Q: What does the man mean?

A. Professor Janson has won a million dollars.

B. Professor Janson is lucky to be teaching at that school.

C. Teachers like Professor Janson are rare.

D. There are a great many teachers of Professor Janson's subject.

* *one in a million* 百萬中選一

rare (rεr) *adj.* 稀少的；罕見的

37. (**D**) M: How's Mary feeling today?

W: She's still running a temperature.

(TONE)

Q: What does the woman say about Mary?

A. She's always running.

B. She's still in the race.

C. She feels very comfortable.

D. She still has a fever.

* *run a temperature* 發燒

38. (**B**) W: How are you doing today?

M: Much better, thanks.

(TONE)

Q: What is the woman asking?

A. How much time the job will take.

B. How the man's health is.

C. What the man is going to do.

D. If the weather is good today.

39. (**C**) W: Have you met our new next-door neighbor?
　　　　 M: What a beautiful car she has!

　　(TONE)
　　Q: What can be concluded about the man?
　　A. He likes to keep his car looking beautiful.
　　B. He wonders who their next neighbor will be.
　　C. He admires the neighbor's car.
　　D. He hasn't met the new neighbor yet.

　　* admire〔əd'maɪr〕v. 羨慕;讚賞

40. (**C**) W: Would you like a cup of coffee to help you wake up?
　　　　 M: A cup of coffee? I'll need three or four.

　　(TONE)
　　Q: What does the man mean?
　　A. He needs to sleep for three or four hours.
　　B. He wants to buy a set of coffee cups.
　　C. He will need more than one cup of coffee.
　　D. He has been wide awake for some time.

　　* *wide awake* 清醒的　　*some time* 一段時間

41. (**D**) M: What does this word mean?
　　　　 W: Don't you have a dictionary?

　　(TONE)
　　Q: What does the woman mean?
　　A. She wants to borrow his dictionary.
　　B. She doesn't know which word he means.
　　C. He shouldn't use such big words.
　　D. He should look the word up in a dictionary.

　　* *look up* 查閱

42. (**B**)　W: You want another sandwich?
　　　M: Yeah, I usually eat a lot when I'm nervous.

　　　(TONE)
　　　Q: What does the man mean?
　　　A. He gets nervous when he goes to dinner parties.
　　　B. He eats when he needs to calm down.
　　　C. He thinks the other sandwich would be much better.
　　　D. He wants the woman to eat the rest of the food.
　　　* *calm down* 冷靜

43. (**C**)　W: Have you met Marge yet?
　　　M: We're from the same hometown.

　　　(TONE)
　　　Q: What does the man mean?
　　　A. Marge has gone home.
　　　B. Marge feels at home there.
　　　C. He's known Marge for a long time.
　　　D. He just met Marge.

44. (**B**)　W: Why did Shelley go to Iowa?
　　　M: Who knows?

　　　(TONE)
　　　Q: What does the man mean?
　　　A. Shelley knows someone there.
　　　B. Shelley didn't tell him.
　　　C. He doesn't know who Shelley is.
　　　D. He wonders which way Shelley went.

45. (**A**)　W: Do you think it'll rain?
　　　M: Rain, it's about to pour!

(TONE)

Q: What does the man mean?

A. There will be a lot of rain.

B. Rain is very unlikely.

C. It's already raining.

D. She's not sure.

* pour (por) v. 下傾盆大雨

Part D

46. (**A**) I don't understand why Andy got food poisoning yesterday.
The doctor says the illness is a result of eating improperly
canned food. I think he is expected to recover soon.

(TONE)

Q: What caused Andy's illness?

A. He ate spoiled food.

B. He ate uncooked food.

C. He didn't cook food long enough.

D. He ate food just gotten out of the oven.

* ***food poisoning*** 食物中毒　　improperly (ɪm'prɑpəlɪ) adv. 不適當地
canned food 罐頭食品　　spoiled (spɔɪld) adj. 腐壞的
oven ('ʌvən) n. 烤箱

47. (**D**) Balloons have been used for sport for about a hundred years.
There are two kinds of sport balloons: gas and hot air. Hot air
balloons are safer than gas balloons, which may catch fire.

(TONE)

Q: What type of balloon is this speaker referring to?

A. Children's play balloons.

B. Weather balloons.

C. Balloons used for safety patrols.

D. Balloons used for recreation.

* balloon (bə'lun) n. 氣球　　***catch fire*** 著火
refer to 意指　　patrol (pə'trol) n. 巡邏

48. (**C**) Helen Keller was born a healthy, normal child in Alabama in 1880. However, an illness accompanied by a high fever struck her while she was still an infant, leaving her deaf, blind, and unable to speak.

(TONE)

Q: Why was Helen Keller blind, deaf, and unable to speak?

A. Because she'd been born that way.

B. Because a horse had kicked her.

C. Because she'd had a very high fever.

D. Because she'd had a bad fall.

　* accompany〔ə'kʌmpənɪ〕v. 伴隨
　　infant〔'ɪnfənt〕n. 嬰兒

49. (**A**) May I have the attention of all students? We are going to take the swimming test. Please take a card and put your name on it. Everyone must swim at least 50 yards to pass. Those of you who want to sail must swim a hundred yards.

(TONE)

Q: What is the minimum distance required to pass the test?

A. Fifty yards.

B. Fifty laps.

C. Once around the yard.

D. One length of the pool.

　* sail〔sel〕v. 航行　　minimum〔'mɪnəməm〕adj. 最小的；最短的
　　require〔rɪ'kwaɪr〕v. 需要　　lap〔læp〕n.（游泳池）一趟來回
　　yard〔jɑrd〕n. 碼；院子　　length〔lɛŋ(k)θ〕n. 一趟

50. (**C**) Stephen A. Douglas was the name of the candidate defeated by Abraham Lincoln in the 1860 presidential race. Nicknamed the "Little Giant," Douglas was short in stature but had a large head and shoulders.

(TONE)

Q: Why was Douglas called the "Little Giant"?

A. Because he felt strongly about slavery.

B. Because he was defeated by Lincoln for president.

C. Because he was short in stature but strong in frame.

D. Because his head was larger than his shoulders.

* candidate ('kændədɪt) *n.* 候選人
nickname ('nɪk,nem) *v.* 暱稱；取綽號
stature ('stætʃə) *n.* 身材　　slavery ('slevərɪ) *n.* 奴隸制度
frame (frem) *n.* 體格

51. (**A**) Good morning, and welcome to American studies 101. I would like to begin this semester by discussing the region of the United States known as the Northeast. This region includes twelve states and a small area called the District of Columbia that is the home of the national government.

(TONE)

Q: When is the lecture probably being given?

A. On the first day of class.

B. At the end of the first week of classes.

C. Halfway through the semester.

D. Just before the final exam.

* district ('dɪstrɪkt) *n.* 地區
the District of Columbia 哥倫比亞特區

52. (**C**) Among the most enthralling of storytellers, Guy de Maupassant is one of the few great French writers who need little interpretation. There is nothing vague about his writing. And as Conrad observed, he is never dull.

(TONE)

Q: What nationality was de Maupassant?

A. Russian.

B. German.

C. French.

D. Polish.

* enthralling (ɪn'θrɔlɪŋ) *adj.* 迷人的
  interpretation (ɪn,tɜ˞prɪ'teʃən) *n.* 解釋   vague (veg) *adj.* 模糊的
  nationality (,næʃən'ælətɪ) *n.* 國籍   Polish ('polɪʃ) *n.* 波蘭人

53. (**C**) Partly cloudy today through Thursday with a chance of afternoon and evening thunderstorms.　A 30 percent chance of rain today and Thursday, 20 percent chance tonight.

(TONE)

Q: According to the report, how is the weather going to be?

A. Cool.

B. Warm.

C. Cloudy.

D. Sunny.

54. (**A**) Hello, I'm Harold Smith.　As the editor of "The Voice", I'd like to introduce you to our campus daily.　We need volunteers to assist us in keeping the student body informed through our newspaper.

(TONE)

Q: Who is Harold Smith?

A. The editor.

B. A journalism professor.

C. The budget director.

D. An engineer.

* daily ('delɪ) *n.* 日報   assist (ə'sɪst) *v.* 幫助
  body ('badɪ) *n.* 團體   informed (ɪn'fɔrmd) *adj.* 消息靈通的
  journalism ('dʒɜ˞nəl,ɪzəm) *n.* 新聞學   budget ('bʌdʒɪt) *n.* 預算

55. (**B**) Before we move on to the next laboratory, I want to explain what we are doing at this point in our research procedure. In the tank area of the lab, my assistants are working with one species of fish, in this case it's salmon.

(TONE)
Q: What is the speaker's field of work?
A. Commercial fishing.
B. Biology.
C. Mechanical engineering.
D. Computer programming.

* ***move on to*** 進行到~   procedure (prə'sidʒɚ) *n.* 程序
   tank (tæŋk) *n.* 水槽   assistant (ə'sɪstənt) *n.* 助手
   salmon ('sælmən) *n.* 鮭魚   biology (baɪ'ɑlədʒɪ) *n.* 生物學

56. (**C**) For the past few weeks we have been discussing national energy conservation alternatives for the future.　Today, I am going to talk about what one community is presently doing to conserve energy.　The people of Davis, California have succeeded in cutting their energy consumption by one-third since 1973.

(TONE)
Q: What is the main topic of this lecture?
A. Bicycles and cars.
B. Building codes.
C. Energy conservation.
D. New housing construction.

* ***energy conservation*** 節約能源   alternative (ɔl'tɜnətɪv) *n.* 選擇
   consumption (kən'sʌmpʃən) *n.* 消耗量

57. (**A**) Today it's my turn to give the weekly oral report.　And the topic that Professor May has assigned me is the life of the poet, Emily Dickinson.　Compared to Walt Whitman who we discussed last week, I found Emily Dickinson is strikingly different.

(TONE)

Q: What is the main topic of the man's report?

A. The life of Emily Dickinson.

B. The poetry of Walt Whitman.

C. The work of Professor May.

D. The life of Walt Whitman.

  * oral ('ɔrəl) *adj.* 口頭的　　strikingly ('straɪkɪŋlɪ) *adv.* 明顯地

58. (**A**) Welcome to our city.　I'm glad you can all take a break from your studies long enough to spend a few hours with us touring the city.　We'll see lots of interesting sights today ranging from famous landmarks to some little-known and out-of-the-way places that most tourists never see.

(TONE)

Q: Who is the man speaking to?

A. Students.

B. Government officials.

C. City planners.

D. Fishermen.

  * ***out-of-the-way*** 偏僻的

59. (**D**) After spring vacation, I expect you to turn in your completed research paper.　As you know, you may write on any novelist who lived between 1850 and 1900.　I assume you have gone to the library already and looked for books containing information about your subject.

(TONE)

Q: When does this talk take place?

A. After class.

B. At the beginning of the term.

C. In the fall.

D. Before vacation.

  * ***turn in*** 繳交

60. (**A**) The total defeat of the Spanish Armada in 1588 is a major problem in European history. Some scholars have suggested that the sinking of the Spanish caused the decline of the Spanish empire and the rise of the British.

(TONE)

Q: When did the defeat of the Spanish Armada take place?

A. 1588.

B. 1603.

C. 1683.

D. 1688.

* armada (ɑr'mɑdə) *n.* 艦隊   decline (dɪ'klaɪn) *n.* 衰亡
empire ('ɛmpaɪr) *n.* 帝國

English Listening Comprehension Test

Test Book No. 2

This listening comprehension test will test your ability to understand spoken English. In this test, each conversation, statement and question will be spoken JUST ONE TIME. They will not be written out for you. There are four parts to this test. Special instructions will be given to you at the beginning of each part.

Part A

In Part A, you will see several pictures in your test book. For each picture, you will be asked 1 to 3 questions. For each question, you will hear four possible answers. Choose the best answer according to what you see in the picture.

Example:

You will see:

You will hear: What is this?
  A. This is a table.
  B. This is a chair.
  C. This is a watch.
  D. This is a doll.

The best answer to the question "What is this?" is B: "This is a chair." Therefore, you should choose answer B.

A. <u>Questions 1-3</u>

D. <u>Questions 10-12</u>

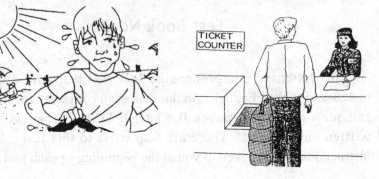

B. <u>Questions 4-6</u>

E. <u>Questions 13-15</u>

C. <u>Questions 7-9</u>

Part B

In Part B, you will hear 15 questions. After you hear a question, read the four possible answers in your test book and decide which one is the best answer to the question you have heard.

Example:

You will hear: What does your father do?

You will read: A. He's 50 years old.
　　　　　　　B. He's a teacher.
　　　　　　　C. He's hungry.
　　　　　　　D. He's in Los Angeles.

The best answer to the question "What does your father do?" is B: "He's a teacher." Therefore, you should choose answer B.

Please go to the next page. ⇨

16. A. Yes, just name it.
    B. Well, it depends.
    C. Certainly. What can I do
       for you?
    D. Yes, of course.
       I wouldn't.

17. A. Many thanks.
    B. I have enough time to go
       shopping.
    C. So am I.
    D. My watch says eleven-
       forty.

18. A. Yes, I was.
    B. No, I did.
    C. Yes, I didn't.
    D. Certainly not.

19. A. Of course, I will.
    B. Thanks. Have one, too.
    C. That's it.
    D. Not at all.

20. A. I'll eat what is here.
    B. Pass me an apple, please.
    C. Thank you. I've had
       enough.
    D. It seems a bit thin.

21. A. Don't thank.
    B. Certainly.
    C. You're welcome.
    D. No thanks.

22. A. In English.
    B. Every four days.
    C. Three days on foot.
    D. A week once.

23. A. I play chess.
    B. I didn't like to watch TV.
    C. Why? Will you play
       tennis with me?
    D. Maybe you know it better
       than I do.

24. A. He comes from his home.
    B. He is American.
    C. He comes from the store.
    D. From Taipei. He is a
       Japanese.

25. A. Where, where.
    B. Thank you.
    C. You're welcome.
    D. Of course.

26. A. Yesterday morning.
    B. Something about my English homework.
    C. Because he knew my father.
    D. You are telling me.

27. A. I'm glad you enjoyed it.
    B. Welcome!
    C. Hope that you can give me one.
    D. No, thanks.

28. A. No, he is.
    B. No, he doesn't.
    C. Yes, he is.
    D. Yes, he does.

29. A. How dreadful!
    B. Better luck next time.
    C. It can't be helped.
    D. How funny.

30. A. Yes, I always have tea for breakfast.
    B. Well, can I get you anything else?
    C. I think many people drink too much.
    D. I'll have the same again, please.

Part C

In Part C, you will hear 15 conversations between a man and a woman. After each conversation, you will hear a question about the conversation. After you hear the question, read the four possible answers in your test book and choose the best answer to the question you have heard.

Example:

You will hear: (Man)   How do you go to school every day?
(Woman) Usually by bus. Sometimes by taxi.

TONE: How does the woman go to school?

You will read: A. She always goes to school on foot.
B. She usually takes a bike.
C. She takes either a bus or a taxi.
D. She usually goes to school by bus, never by taxi.

The best answer to the question "How does the woman go to school?" is C: "She takes either a bus or a taxi." Therefore, you should choose answer C.

Please go to the next page. ⟹

31. A. He has found someone else
    to go to the concert with him.
    B. The woman should have
    contacted him earlier.
    C. He is looking for someone
    to go to the concert with him.
    D. The woman has to find
    someone else to go to the
    concert with.

32. A. He wants to buy film.
    B. He wants to have the pictures
    enlarged.
    C. He wants to get some film
    developed.
    D. He wants a negative to be
    printed.

33. A. He wants to get medicine.
    B. He wants to fill out the
    prescription.
    C. He wants to get information
    on a prescription.
    D. He wants to see a doctor.

34. A. She hasn't talked with the
    manager yet.
    B. The new manager was not
    in the office.
    C. The woman has been at home.
    D. The woman didn't want to
    talk with the new manager.

35. A. She wants him to go to
    the office now.
    B. She wants him to wait.
    C. She wants him to hang up
    the phone.
    D. She wants him to come
    back at three.

36. A. Hang up the phone.
    B. Call her friend
    immediately.
    C. Get the telephone right
    now.
    D. Pass the CPA exam as
    Bob did.

37. A. On the table in the living
    room.
    B. In the man's office.
    C. In the living room.
    D. At Bob's home.

38. A. Put the sofa on the stereo.
    B. Move the sofa.
    C. Take the sofa out of the
    room.
    D. Buy a smaller sofa.

39. A. Asking some other people to help with the move instead of him.
    B. Finding a different apartment.
    C. Trying to find others to help her too.
    D. Asking club members to find some other apartment.

40. A. She is confident of passing the test.
    B. She is not really ready but she thinks she will pass the test.
    C. She is not really a good student but she will pass the test.
    D. She is ready for the test and will get good grades.

41. A. Stop at the grocery store.
    B. Use them in his office.
    C. Take them with him for lunch.
    D. Borrow them from his neighbor.

42. A. He is coming down with a cold, so he doesn't want to go.
    B. He is no longer ill but he wants to take care of himself.
    C. He wants to give a new flute to Susan, so he will go to the party.
    D. He doesn't want to go because he wants to practice the flute.

43. A. To make a room reservation.
    B. To pack many items in a box.
    C. To cancel the plane tickets for two.
    D. To put one small item in her suitcase.

44. A. The woman may have made a mistake.
    B. The woman actually saw the singer.
    C. The woman thought the singer is in town.
    D. The woman should go to San Francisco.

45. A. Mary may not come to the party.
    B. Probably Mary will invite the woman first.
    C. Mary will probably come to the woman's party.
    D. The man will ask Mary to go to the party.

Part D

In Part D, you will hear 15 short talks. After each talk, you will hear a question about the talk. After you hear the question, read the four possible answers in your test book and choose the best answer to the question you have heard.

Example:

You will hear: Well, that's all for Unit 15. For today's homework, please do the review questions on page 80, and we'll check the answers tomorrow. Now, let's go on to Unit 16.

TONE: What is the teacher going to do next in today's class?

You will read: A. Check the homework.
B. Review Unit 15.
C. Start a new unit.
D. Answer students' questions.

The best answer to the question "What is the teacher going to do next in today's class?" is C: "Start a new unit." Therefore, you should choose answer C.

Please go to the next page. ⇨

46. A. 1920.
    B. 1928.
    C. 1950.
    D. 1955.

47. A. It is close to the coastline.
    B. It has good soil.
    C. It has a large labor supply.
    D. It has the proper climate.

48. A. A magazine.
    B. A neighborhood.
    C. A period of time.
    D. A political issue.

49. A. Christmas.
    B. New Year's Day.
    C. Easter.
    D. The summer solstice.

50. A. By supporting conservation laws.
    B. By using them frequently.
    C. By using their natural resources.
    D. By increasing their animal populations.

51. A. Mr. Rockford.
    B. Mr. Rockford's friend.
    C. The receptionist.
    D. Mr. Rockford's boss.

52. A. It is self-service.
    B. It is cheap.
    C. It is high quality.
    D. It is available in schools.

53. A. At a residence.
    B. From his local fire department.
    C. From Underwriters' Laboratories.
    D. At a hardware store.

54. A. Workers may not smoke while they work.
    B. Workers may not smoke in the factory.
    C. Workers may only smoke in certain places in the factory.
    D. Workers may only smoke in certain places outside the factory.

55. A. A locksmith.
    B. A car rental agency.
    C. A gas station.
    D. A bookstore.

56. A. The regular staff.
    B. Hotel guests.
    C. Temporary workers.
    D. Female customers.

57. A. On Flight 437.
    B. In Montreal.
    C. At an airport.
    D. In a park.

58. A. On a train.
    B. In a park.
    C. On a platform.
    D. In a store.

59. A. A member of the Blasters.
    B. A radio DJ.
    C. A Romance Records spokesman.
    D. A movie star.

60. A. An insurance company.
    B. A travel agency.
    C. A golf course.
    D. A news agency.

Listening Test 2 詳解

Part A

For questions number 1 to 3, please look at picture A.

1. (**B**) Question number 1, what is the boy doing?
    A. He is swimming.
    B. He is sweating.
    C. He is washing his hands.
    D. He is drinking.

2. (**A**) Question number 2, please look at picture A again. Where is the boy?
    A. He is at the beach.
    B. He is in a park.
    C. He is at a swimming pool.
    D. He is on a bench.

3. (**D**) Question number 3, please look at picture A again. How is the weather?
    A. It is warm.
    B. It is stormy.
    C. It is muggy.
    D. It is hot.

    * stormy ('stɔrmɪ) *adj.* 暴風雨的   muggy ('mʌgɪ) *adj.* 悶熱的

For questions number 4 to 6, please look at picture B.

4. (**C**) Question number 4, what is the season?
    A. It is spring.
    B. It is summer.
    C. It is fall.
    D. It is winter.

5. (**B**) Question number 5, please look at picture B again.　What is the man on the left side doing?

    A. He is sweeping leaves.

    B. He is raking leaves.

    C. He is picking leaves.

    D. He is pulling leaves.

    * rake (rek) *v.* 鏟

6. (**B**) Question number 6, please look at picture B again.　How is the weather?

    A. It is hot.

    B. It is cool.

    C. It is frigid.

    D. It is windy.

    * frigid ('frɪdʒɪd) *adj.* 寒冷的

For questions number 7 to 9, please look at picture C.

7. (**D**) Question number 7, how is the weather?

    A. It is humid.

    B. It is clear.

    C. It is cloudy.

    D. It is rainy.

    * humid ('hjumɪd) *adj.* 潮濕的

8. (**B**) Question number 8, please look at picture C again.　What is the woman on the left side doing?

    A. She is walking in a pool.

    B. She is walking in a puddle.

    C. She is walking in a hole.

    D. She is walking in a river.

    * puddle ('pʌdl̩) *n.* 水坑

9. (**A**) Question number 9, please look at picture C again. What is the pattern of the umbrella in front?

   A. It is striped.
   B. It is floral.
   C. It is polka-dot.
   D. It is a solid color.

   * striped (straɪpt) *adj.* 有斑紋的　　floral ('florəl) *adj.* 花的
   　polka-dot 圓點花樣　　*solid color* 純色

For questions number 10 to 12, please look at picture D.

10. (**C**) Question number 10, where is the man?

   A. He is in a movie theater.
   B. He is in a hotel.
   C. He is in an airport.
   D. He is in a bank.

11. (**B**) Question number 11, please look at picture D again. What is the man holding?

   A. He is holding a ticket.
   B. He is holding a baggage.
   C. He is holding an umbrella.
   D. He is holding a box.

12. (**B**) Question number 12, please look at picture D again. What is the man doing?

   A. He is checking out.
   B. He is checking in.
   C. He is buying a bag.
   D. He is getting a checkup.

   * *check out* 結帳離開　　*check in* 登記報到
   　checkup ('tʃɛk,ʌp) *n.* (健康) 檢查

For questions number 13 to 15, please look at picture E.

13. (**C**) Question number 13, where are these people?
   A. They are in a bus.
   B. They are in a movie theater.
   C. They are in an airplane.
   D. They are in a hotel.

14. (**C**) Question number 14, please look at picture E again. What is the flight attendant on the right doing?
   A. She is helping a sick woman.
   B. She is reading.
   C. He is serving drinks.
   D. He is walking.
   * *flight attendant* 空服員·

15. (**D**) Question number 15, please look at picture E again. What is the passenger on the left doing?
   A. She is seasick.
   B. She is fainting.
   C. She is crying.
   D. She is getting airsick.
   * seasick ('si,sɪk) *adj.* 暈船的   faint (fent) *v.* 暈倒
   airsick ('ɛr,sɪk) *adj.* 暈機的

Part B

16. (**B**) Would you mind doing me a favor?
   A. Yes, just name it.
   B. Well, it depends.
   C. Certainly. What can I do for you?
   D. Yes, of course. I wouldn't.
   * *It depends.* 看情況而定。

17. (**D**) What time do you have?　My watch doesn't work.
   A. Many thanks.
   B. I have enough time to go shopping.
   C. So am I.
   D. My watch says eleven-forty.

18. (**D**) Did you like it?
   A. Yes, I was.
   B. No, I did.
   C. Yes, I didn't.
   D. Certainly not.

19. (**B**) Happy New Year!
   A. Of course, I will.
   B. Thanks.　Have one, too.
   C. That's it.
   D. Not at all.

20. (**D**) How do you find the soup?
   A. I'll eat what is here.
   B. Pass me an apple, please.
   C. Thank you.　I've had enough.
   D. It seems a bit thin.

   * thin〔θɪn〕adj. 味淡的

21. (**C**) Thank you for opening the door.
   A. Don't thank.
   B. Certainly.
   C. You're welcome.
   D. No thanks.

22. (**B**) How often do you write to your parents?
　　A. In English.
　　B. Every four days.
　　C. Three days on foot.
　　D. A week once.
　　* *on foot* 徒步

23. (**A**) What do you do in your free time?
　　A. I play chess.
　　B. I didn't like to watch TV.
　　C. Why?　Will you play tennis with me?
　　D. Maybe you know it better than I do.
　　* *free time* 空閒時間　　chess〔tʃɛs〕*n.* 西洋棋

24. (**B**) Where does he come from?
　　A. He comes from his home.
　　B. He is American.
　　C. He comes from the store.
　　D. From Taipei.　He is a Japanese.
　　* come from 用現在式，表示「籍貫、出生於」。

25. (**B**) You are a very good student.
　　A. Where, where.
　　B. Thank you.
　　C. You're welcome.
　　D. Of course.
　　* 英文中沒有 where, where. 的說法。

26. (**B**) What did your teacher tell you?
　　A. Yesterday morning.
　　B. Something about my English homework.
　　C. Because he knew my father.
　　D. You are telling me.
　　* *You are telling me.* 還用你說。（我早就知道了。）

27. (**A**) I've got to leave. Thanks for a pleasant evening.
        A. I'm glad you enjoyed it.
        B. Welcome!
        C. Hope that you can give me one.
        D. No, thanks.

28. (**C**) He is a good man, isn't he?
        A. No, he is.
        B. No, he doesn't.
        C. Yes, he is.
        D. Yes, he does.

29. (**B**) I failed to get the prize.
        A. How dreadful!
        B. Better luck next time.
        C. It can't be helped.
        D. How funny.

        * *fail to* 未能   dreadful (ˈdrɛdfəl) *adj.* 可怕的
        It can't be helped. 誰都無能爲力。

30. (**D**) What would you like to drink?
        A. Yes, I always have tea for breakfast.
        B. Well, can I get you anything else?
        C. I think many people drink too much.
        D. I'll have the same again, please.

Part C

31. (**B**) W: I won't be able to go to the concert with you tonight.
        M: That's too bad, but I wish you would have told me sooner
        so I could have found someone else to go with.

(TONE)

Q: What is the man telling the woman?

A. He has found someone else to go to the concert with him.

B. The woman should have contacted him earlier.

C. He is looking for someone to go to the concert with him.

D. The woman has to find someone else to go to the concert with.

32. (**C**) M: Would you develop this roll?

W: All right.　That will be $7.

(TONE)

Q: What does the man want?

A. He wants to buy film.

B. He wants to have the pictures enlarged.

C. He wants to get some film developed.

D. He wants a negative to be printed.

* develop (dɪ'vɛləp) v. 沖洗 (底片)　　roll (rol) n. 一捲 (底片)
enlarge (ɪn'lɑrdʒ) v. 放大　　negative ('nɛgətɪv) n. (照相機) 負片

33. (**A**) W: May I help you?

M: I'd like to get this prescription filled.

(TONE)

Q: What does the man want?

A. He wants to get medicine.

B. He wants to fill out the prescription.

C. He wants to get information on a prescription.

D. He wants to see a doctor.

* prescription (prɪ'skrɪpʃən) n. 處方　　***fill out*** 填寫

34. (**A**) M: Did you talk with our new manager?

W: I have been out of town for two days.

(TONE)

Q: What does the woman mean?

A. She hasn't talked with the manager yet.

B. The new manager was not in the office.

C. The woman has been at home.

D. The woman didn't want to talk with the new manager.

35. (**B**) M: I have an appointment with the Dean of Students at two o'clock.

W: He is on the phone now, so why don't you have a seat?

(TONE)

Q: What does the woman want the man to do?

A. She wants him to go to the office now.

B. She wants him to wait.

C. She wants him to hang up the phone.

D. She wants him to come back at three.

* *hang up* 掛斷

36. (**A**) M: Get off the phone Susan. I am expecting a phone call from one of my clients.

W: Wait. I am talking to Bob who passed the CPA exam.

(TONE)

Q: What does the man want Susan to do?

A. Hang up the phone.

B. Call her friend immediately.

C. Get the telephone right now.

D. Pass the CPA exam as Bob did.

* client ('klaɪənt) *n.* 客戶

   CPA 美國合格會計師 (= *Certified Public Accountant*)

37. (**D**) W: Do you know what happened to the National Geographic
Magazine?

M: I know it was on the table in the living room, but Bob
borrowed it this morning.

(TONE)

Q: Where is the magazine now?

A. On the table in the living room.

B. In the man's office.

C. In the living room.

D. At Bob's home.

* *National Geographic Magazine* 國家地理雜誌

38. (**B**) M: Mrs. Smith, should I put the sofa right here, next to this
stereo set?

W: Oh, I guess it's all right, but more to the side please if
you will.

(TONE)

Q: What does the woman think he should do?

A. Put the sofa on the stereo.

B. Move the sofa.

C. Take the sofa out of the room.

D. Buy a smaller sofa.

* *stereo set* 立體音響

39. (**C**) W: I can't stay in this apartment because the rent went up very
high, so I am going to move out next week. Do you think
you can give me a hand?

M: Don't worry. I'll ask my club members and see if some of
them are free also.

(TONE)

Q: What does the man suggest?

A. Asking some other people to help with the move instead of him.

B. Finding a different apartment.

C. Trying to find others to help her too.

D. Asking club members to find some other apartment.

* rent ﹝ rɛnt ﹞ *n.* 租金　　***give sb. a hand*** 幫助某人

40. (**B**) M: How are your studies coming?　Do you think you are ready for the test?

W: Not really, but I guess I'll make it all right.

(TONE)

Q: What does the woman mean?

A. She is confident of passing the test.

B. She is not really ready but she thinks she will pass the test.

C. She is not really a good student but she will pass the test.

D. She is ready for the test and will get good grades.

41. (**A**) W: I ran out of both salt and pepper.

M: I'll pick them up on my way home from work.

(TONE)

Q: What will the man probably do?

A. Stop at the grocery store.

B. Use them in his office.

C. Take them with him for lunch.

D. Borrow them from his neighbor.

* ***run out of*** 用完　　salt ﹝ sɔlt ﹞ *n.* 鹽
pepper (ˈpɛpɚ) *n.* 胡椒粉
pick up 買得　　***grocery store*** 雜貨店

42. (**B**) W: Are you coming to Susan's birthday party at my house?

M: I'll see, because I've just gotten over the flu.

(TONE)

Q: What does the man mean?

A. He is coming down with a cold, so he doesn't want to go.

B. He is no longer ill but he wants to take care of himself.

C. He wants to give a new flute to Susan, so he will go to the party.

D. He doesn't want to go because he wants to practice the flute.

* ***get over*** 自~痊癒　　flu (flu) *n.* 流行性感冒
come down with 染上~（病）　　flute (flut) *n.* 長笛

43. (**D**) M: Do you have room for this small one?

W: Let me see.　Oh maybe I could squeeze it in my cosmetic case.

(TONE)

Q: What is the man asking the woman?

A. To make a room reservation.

B. To pack many items in a box.

C. To cancel the plane tickets for two.

D. To put one small item in her suitcase.

* squeeze (skwiz) *v.* 把~塞入　　***cosmetic case*** 化妝箱
make a room reservation 預定房間　　item ('aɪtəm) *n.* 物件

44. (**A**) W: Guess what!　I saw John Smith, the rock singer in a downtown restaurant today.

M: You thought it was him, but he is supposed to be in San Francisco for his concert tour.

(TONE)

Q: What does the man imply?

A. The woman may have made a mistake.

B. The woman actually saw the singer.

C. The woman thought the singer is in town.

D. The woman should go to San Francisco.

* rock〔rɑk〕n. 搖滾樂　　downtown〔͵daʊn'taʊn〕adj. 市中心的
concert tour 巡迴演唱

45. (**C**) W: I heard Mary has been invited to another dinner party,
　　　　　 but I'm sure I invited her first.

　　　　 M: Well, she is more likely to attend your party than the
　　　　　 other one.

(TONE)

Q: What does the man mean?

A. Mary may not come to the party.

B. Probably Mary will invite the woman first.

C. Mary will probably come to the woman's party.

D. The man will ask Mary to go to the party.

* attend〔ə'tɛnd〕v. 參加

Part D

46. (**A**) Walt Disney started creating cartoon animations in 1920, but
　　　　 it was 1928 when his best known character, Mickey Mouse,
　　　　 came to life.

(TONE)

Q: In which year did Walt Disney first begin creating cartoon
　 animations?

A. 1920.

B. 1928.

C. 1950.

D. 1955.

* **cartoon animation** 卡通動畫　　**come to life** 誕生

47. (**D**) Few regions in the world produce raisins since the growers must have many weeks of hot, rainless weather in which to dry the grapes.　Parts of Southern California are ideal for cultivating these grapes since the period from August to November there is hot and dry.

(TONE)
Q: Why is Southern California a large raisin-producing area?
A. It is close to the coastline.
B. It has good soil.
C. It has a large labor supply.
D. It has the proper climate.

* region ('ridʒən) *n.* 地區　　raisin ('rezn̩) *n.* 葡萄乾
grape (grep) *n.* 葡萄　　cultivate ('kʌltə,vet) *v.* 耕種
coastline ('kost,laɪn) *n.* 海岸線　　soil (sɔɪl) *n.* 土壤

48. (**A**) The periodical "Masses" covered not only the people and life of Greenwich Village, but also hot political topics that were rarely spoken of by most Americans during the prewar years.

(TONE)
Q: What is the topic of this talk?
A. A magazine.
B. A neighborhood.
C. A period of time.
D. A political issue.

* periodical (,pɪrɪ'ɑdɪkl̩) *n.* 期刊
Greenwich Village ('grɛnɪtʃ'vɪlɪdʒ) *n.* (紐約市) 格林威治村
prewar (pri'wɔr) *adj.* 戰前的　　issue ('ɪʃju) *n.* 議題

49. (**C**) One note to consider here is that most people associate *The Messiah* with Christmas; but, this was not what Handel intended.　He wrote *The Messiah* to be performed in the spring, just before Easter.

(TONE)

Q: What celebration was this musical work intended for?

A. Christmas.

B. New Year's Day.

C. Easter.

D. The summer solstice.

* associate (ə'soʃɪˌet) v. 使結合 (*with*)　　Easter ('istə) n. 復活節
summer solstice 夏至

50. (**A**) If we want to continue to enjoy our open spaces in woodlands, then we must support conservation legislation and join local organizations which promote these laws.

(TONE)

Q: How can we preserve open spaces in woodlands?

A. By supporting conservation laws.

B. By using them frequently.

C. By using their natural resources.

D. By increasing their animal populations.

* *open space* 空地　　woodland ('wʊdˌlænd) n. 林地
conservation (ˌkɑnsə'veʃən) n. 保育
legislation (ˌlɛdʒɪs'leʃən) n. 立法　　local ('lokḷ) adj. 當地的
organization (ˌɔrgənə'zeʃən) n. 組織　　promote (prə'mot) v. 促動

51. (**C**) Paging Mr. Edward Rockford.　Would Mr. Edward Rockford please come to the reception desk?

(TONE)

Q: Who is speaking?

A. Mr. Rockford.

B. Mr. Rockford's friend.

C. The receptionist.

D. Mr. Rockford's boss.

* page (pedʒ) v. 呼叫　　*reception desk* 接待櫃台
receptionist (rɪ'sɛpʃənɪst) n. 接待員

52. (**B**) Self-service style, or cafeteria style, as it is sometimes called, is used at many schools and companies. The food is served quickly and is inexpensive. However, food quality sometimes suffers.

(TONE)

Q: What is an advantage of cafeteria-style food?

A. It is self-service.
B. It is cheap.
C. It is high quality.
D. It is available in schools.

* cafeteria (ˌkæfə'tırıə) *n.* 自助餐廳　　suffer ('sʌfə) *v.* 受損

53. (**D**) With the ever increasing threat of home fires, Americans are choosing smoke alarm systems which can be easily installed as warning devices in residences. Smoke alarm systems are listed by Underwriters' Laboratories and can be bought at hardware stores.

(TONE)

Q: Where can a homeowner obtain a fire alarm system for his residence?

A. At a residence.
B. From his local fire department.
C. From Underwriters' Laboratories.
D. At a hardware store.

* install (ın'stɔl) *v.* 安裝　　residence ('rɛzədəns) *n.* 住宅
hardware store 五金行　　homeowner ('hom‚onə) *n.* 屋主

54. (**C**) Attention, please. Smoking is not allowed in the factory, except in designated areas.

(TONE)

Q: What does this announcement mean?

A. Workers may not smoke while they work.

B. Workers may not smoke in the factory.

C. Workers may only smoke in certain places in the factory.

D. Workers may only smoke in certain places outside the factory.

* designated (ˈdɛzɪɡˌnetɪd) *adj.* 指定的

55. (**B**) Leave the keys in the car. Do not lock the doors. Note your mileage and gas. Take all personal belongings with you. Attendants can give you a receipt in the parking lot.

(TONE)

Q: What kind of company is this?

A. A locksmith.

B. A car rental agency.

C. A gas station.

D. A bookstore.

* mileage (ˈmaɪlɪdʒ) *n.* 哩數   attendant (əˈtɛndənt) *n.* 服務人員
receipt (rɪˈsit) *n.* 收據   *parking lot* 停車場
locksmith (ˈlɑkˌsmɪθ) *n.* 鎖店
car rental agency 租車中心   *gas station* 加油站

56. (**A**) The total eclipse of the sun on Thursday next week has dramatically increased bookings. Every room will be filled with every cot in use to give us the maximum number of beds. Many of our guests are making their first visit to the city. Extra workers from the town will join us in the kitchen and dining rooms.

(TONE)
Q: Who is this announcement for?
A. The regular staff.
B. Hotel guests.
C. Temporary workers.
D. Female customers.
* eclipse (ɪˋklɪps) n. 蝕　　booking (ˋbʊkɪŋ) n. 預約　　cot (kɑt) n. 摺疊床
regular staff 全體正規職員　　temporary (ˋtɛmpə͵rɛrɪ) adj. 臨時的

57. (**C**) This is the final boarding call for Flight 437 to Montreal.
Any passenger who has not yet boarded should proceed
immediately to Gate 48.　The gate will be closing momentarily.

(TONE)
Q: Where is the speaker?
A. On Flight 437.
B. In Montreal.
C. At an airport.
D. In a park.
* boarding (ˋbɔrdɪŋ) n. 登機　　proceed (prəˋsid) v. 前進
momentarily (ˋmomən͵tɛrəlɪ) adv. 隨時地

58. (**A**) Due to a derailment at Green River Station, this F Line train is
only running as far as Park Boulevard.　For passengers headed
for the Trans-River, change to the Uptown Local at Park
Boulevard and get off at Merchants' Square.　From there, take
the S Line.

(TONE)
Q: Where would this announcement be heard?
A. On a train.
B. In a park.
C. On a platform.
D. In a store.
* ***due to*** 由於　　derailment (diˋrelmənt) n. (列車) 出軌
Uptown Local 市郊列車　　platform (ˋplæt͵fɔrm) n. 月臺

59. (**B**) The Blasters canceled their concert at Chester Auditorium. They said they didn't have a strong base of fans in our area. This station loves their music. Write Romance Records and let them know Taipei is Blasters' country.

(TONE)

Q: Who is speaking?

A. A member of the Blasters.
B. A radio DJ.
C. A Romance Records spokesman.
D. A movie star.

* auditorium (ˌɔdəˈtorɪəm) *n.* 禮堂
　fan (fæn) *n.* (歌曲、運動、電影等) 迷
　DJ 唱片音樂節目廣播員 (= *disk jockey*)

60. (**A**) Enjoy beautiful Padre Island in the Gulf of Mexico! If you buy a whole life policy with Gulf Life, you'll also get a week's vacation for the entire family. Contact Gulf Life and find out about the Padre Island vacation.

(TONE)

Q: What kind of company is this?

A. An insurance company.
B. A travel agency.
C. A golf course.
D. A news agency.

* gulf (gʌlf) *n.* 海灣　　*life policy* 壽險
　insurance (ɪnˈʃʊrəns) *n.* 保險

English Listening Comprehension Test

Test Book No. 3

This listening comprehension test will test your ability to understand spoken English. In this test, each conversation, statement and question will be spoken JUST ONE TIME. They will not be written out for you. There are four parts to this test. Special instructions will be given to you at the beginning of each part.

Part A

In Part A, you will see several pictures in your test book. For each picture, you will be asked 1 to 3 questions. For each question, you will hear four possible answers. Choose the best answer according to what you see in the picture.

Example:

You will see:

You will hear: What is this?
A. This is a table.
B. This is a chair.
C. This is a watch.
D. This is a doll.

The best answer to the question "What is this?" is B: "This is a chair." Therefore, you should choose answer B.

A. Questions 1-2

C. Question 5

B. Questions 3-4

D. Questions 6-7

E. Questions 8-9

G. Questions 11-12

F. Question 10

H. Questions 13-15

Part B

In Part B, you will hear 15 questions.　After you hear a question, read the four possible answers in your test book and decide which one is the best answer to the question you have heard.

Example:

<u>You will hear:</u>　What does your father do?

<u>You will read:</u>　A. He's 50 years old.
　　　　　　　　　　B. He's a teacher.
　　　　　　　　　　C. He's hungry.
　　　　　　　　　　D. He's in Los Angeles.

The best answer to the question "What does your father do?" is B: "He's a teacher."　Therefore, you should choose answer B.

Please go to the next page. ⇨

16. A. Yes, he sometimes eats at his friend's house.
　　B. No, he always does.
　　C. Yes, he sometimes eats at home.
　　D. No, he sometimes eats at a restaurant.

17. A. I'm sorry to hear that.
　　B. All right.
　　C. Because he is very busy.
　　D. No, he can't.

18. A. You can take a city bus.
　　B. That's a good idea.
　　C. Give me a hand.
　　D. That's too bad.

19. A. It's summer.
　　B. It's Monday.
　　C. It's hot.
　　D. It's July 9.

20. A. Do you like seeing movies?
　　B. So do I.
　　C. Neither do I.
　　D. I don't think so.

21. A. Don't give up now.
　　B. Have a good time.
　　C. No, I'm too tired.
　　D. I can't find it.

22. A. Certainly not. I am glad to help you.
　　B. Of course not. I am glad to.
　　C. Of course. You are very kind.
　　D. No, he can carry it by himself.

23. A. So am I.
　　B. So do I.
　　C. So did I.
　　D. So I was.

24. A. It's up to you.
　　B. Why not?
　　C. Take it easy.
　　D. That's a good idea.

25. A. That's too bad.
　　B. I hope so.
　　C. There's something special.
　　D. I went to bed very late last night.

26. A. I am looking down in order to look for my dog.
    B. I got bad grades in my tests yesterday.
    C. I have no idea why you look so sad.
    D. I am waiting for a bus.

27. A. They don't understand.
    B. They were in the living room.
    C. They don't like instant soup.
    D. They are swimming.

28. A. Not at all. Thanks.
    B. I'd love to.
    C. What is it about ?
    D. Yes, we will.

29. A. He works very hard.
    B. Young children like watching TV.
    C. That doesn't surprise me.
    D. There's something wrong with my bike.

30. A. Really?
    B. That's not bad.
    C. I don't know.
    D. You are all right.

Part C

In Part C, you will hear 15 conversations between a man and a woman. After each conversation, you will hear a question about the conversation. After you hear the question, read the four possible answers in your test book and choose the best answer to the question you have heard.

Example:

<u>You will hear</u>:   (Man)   How do you go to school every day?
(Woman)   Usually by bus. Sometimes by taxi.

TONE: How does the woman go to school?

<u>You will read</u>:   A. She always goes to school on foot.
B. She usually takes a bike.
C. She takes either a bus or a taxi.
D. She usually goes to school by bus, never by taxi.

The best answer to the question "How does the woman go to school?" is C: "She takes either a bus or a taxi." Therefore, you should choose answer C.

Please go to the next page. ⇨

31. A. In an airplane.
    B. In a restaurant.
    C. In a stadium.
    D. In a movie theater.

32. A. Steve looks good in
       anything.
    B. He knew someone who
       looked like Steve.
    C. He wishes he had a jacket
       like Steve.
    D. Steve should get a new
       jacket.

33. A. Mr. Smith doesn't work
       there anymore.
    B. Mr. Smith has too much
       work.
    C. Mr. Smith is out of the
       building.
    D. Mr. Smith is in a meeting.

34. A. It will be easy.
    B. It was postponed.
    C. He feels lucky.
    D. He's not prepared.

35. A. He was cold.
    B. He was hot.
    C. The air was stale.
    D. The room was old.

36. A. Yesterday.
    B. Two days ago.
    C. Three days ago.
    D. Early last week.

37. A. That the woman come to
       the party.
    B. A date with Barbara.
    C. That the woman cook for
       the party.
    D. A present for Bill.

38. A. She is also a customer.
    B. The vase has already been
       sold.
    C. She is new in town.
    D. The vase is not for sale.

39. A. She should find someone
       who likes children.
    B. She should hire someone
       responsible and
       trustworthy.
    C. She should hire his son.
    D. She should hire his son's
       girlfriend.

40. A. At a buffet.
    B. At a restaurant.
    C. At someone's house.
    D. At a dinner party.

41. A. How Richard traveled.
    B. Where Richard went.
    C. If Richard will go.
    D. How much Richard spent.

42. A. He was held up in traffic.
    B. He had no way to get home.
    C. He was busy at the office.
    D. His car had to be repaired.

43. A. The man can find work in
       the library.
    B. She can't help the man
       because she's working.
    C. She can work without air
       conditioning.
    D. The man can do his work
       elsewhere.

44. A. The team played one
       hour longer yesterday.
    B. The team had better play
       one more game.
    C. The man should join a
       better team.
    D. The man's team is
       improving.

45. A. He looks like he's lost
       weight.
    B. He exercises regularly.
    C. He doesn't eat much.
    D. He told her so.

Part D

In Part D, you will hear 15 short talks. After each talk, you will hear a question about the talk. After you hear the question, read the four possible answers in your test book and choose the best answer to the question you have heard.

Example:

You will hear:　　Well, that's all for Unit 15. For today's homework, please do the review questions on page 80, and we'll check the answers tomorrow. Now, let's go on to Unit 16.

　　　　　　　　TONE:　What is the teacher going to do next in today's class?

You will read:　　A. Check the homework.
　　　　　　　　B. Review Unit 15.
　　　　　　　　C. Start a new unit.
　　　　　　　　D. Answer students' questions.

The best answer to the question "What is the teacher going to do next in today's class?" is C: "Start a new unit." Therefore, you should choose answer C.

Please go to the next page. ⇨

46. A. Once.
    B. Twice.
    C. Three times.
    D. Four times.

47. A. In the lobby.
    B. In the basement.
    C. On the 3rd floor.
    D. On the 4th floor.

48. A. On the bus.
    B. At an airport.
    C. On the plane.
    D. In front of a boarding gate.

49. A. Advisers.
    B. Medical operators.
    C. Travel agents.
    D. Doctors.

50. A. Washington State.
    B. The Pacific Ocean station.
    C. WXYW.
    D. Citizen's Bank.

51. A. Vice-president of the company.
    B. Director of the advertising division.
    C. Professor at a university.
    D. Manager of the company.

52. A. They fished and raised crops.
    B. They cared for the children and raised crops.
    C. They cared for the children and made clothing.
    D. They made clothing and raised animals.

53. A. They worked in sun and rain.
    B. They worked all the year round.
    C. They went out to work even in typhoons.
    D. They worked in all weathers.

54. A. Ten o'clock.
    B. One o'clock.
    C. One-thirty.
    D. Two o'clock.

55. A. Congress was willing to develop a telegraph system.
    B. Congress refused to appropriate money for the purpose.
    C. Congress assisted private corporations to develop the telegraph system.
    D. Congress believed the telegraph system was worthless.

56. A. Raising funds.
    B. Lifting the nation's cultural level.
    C. Establishing free schools.
    D. Training ministers.

57. A. Lack of nutrients.
    B. Snow and ice.
    C. Heat and drought.
    D. Old age.

58. A. Business leadership.
    B. Investment.
    C. History.
    D. Seminar.

59. A. To demonstrate the latest use of computer graphics.
    B. To discuss the possibility of an economic depression.
    C. To explain the workings of the brain.
    D. To dramatize a famous mystery story.

60. A. A driver who got a speeding ticket.
    B. A newspaper editor who wrote this article.
    C. An officer who is directing the crackdown.
    D. A visitor who is traveling.

Listening Test 3 詳解

Part A

For questions number 1 to 2, please look at picture A.

1. (**B**) Question number 1, how many floors does the house have?
   A. It has one floor.
   B. It has two floors.
   C. It has three floors.
   D. It has four floors.
   * floor〔flor〕*n.* 樓層

2. (**B**) Question number 2, please look at picture A again.　What is the father doing?
   A. He is reading a book.
   B. He is mowing the lawn.
   C. He is doing the dishes.
   D. He is watching TV.
   * mow〔mo〕*v.* 割（草）　　lawn〔lɔn〕*n.* 草地　　***do the dishes*** 洗碗

For questions number 3 to 4, please look at picture B.

3. (**A**) Question number 3, what is the grandfather doing?
   A. He is reading a newspaper and smoking a pipe.
   B. He is watching TV.
   C. He is sleeping.
   D. He is cooking.
   * pipe〔paɪp〕*n.* 煙斗

4. (**A**) Question number 4, please look at picture B again.　What time is it?
   A. It's ten o'clock.
   B. It's one o'clock.
   C. It's four o'clock.
   D. It's six o'clock.

For question number 5, please look at picture C.

5. (**A**) Question number 5, what time of the day is it?
        A. It is morning.
        B. It is noon.
        C. It is evening.
        D. It is midnight.

For questions number 6 to 7, please look at picture D.

6. (**B**) Question number 6, where is the little boy?
        A. He is in the kitchen.
        B. He is in the bathtub.
        C. He is in the living room.
        D. He is on the bed.
        * bathtub (ˈbæθ,tʌb) *n.* 浴缸

7. (**D**) Question number 7, please look at picture D again. What is the mother doing?
        A. The mother is cooking.
        B. The mother is reading a book.
        C. The mother is taking a bath.
        D. The mother is washing the boy's hair.

For questions number 8 to 9, please look at picture E.

8. (**A**) Question number 8, what room of the house is this?
        A. This is the kitchen.
        B. This is the living room.
        C. This is the bathroom.
        D. This is the bedroom.

9. (**B**) Question number 9, please look at picture E again. How many people can you see?
        A. Two.
        B. Three.
        C. Four.
        D. Five.

For question number 10, please look at picture F.

10. (**A**) Question number 10, where should you put your bag?
　　　A. I should put my bag on the baggage shelf.
　　　B. I should put my bag on the check-out counter.
　　　C. I should put my bag in the book stacks.
　　　D. I should put my bag in the newspaper rack.

　　　* shelf (ʃɛlf) *n.* 架子　　*check-out counter* 結帳櫃台
　　　stack (stæk) *n.* 堆　　rack (ræk) *n.* 架子

For questions number 11 to 12, please look at picture G.

11. (**A**) Question number 11, what is this a picture of?
　　　A. This is the customer service area of a bank.
　　　B. This is the lobby of a hotel.
　　　C. This is the waiting room of a railroad station.
　　　D. This is the classroom of a school.

　　　* lobby ('labɪ) *n.* 大廳　　*waiting room* 候車室

12. (**B**) Question number 12, please look at picture G again.　Where
　　　do you wait for an available teller?
　　　A. I must wait at the door.
　　　B. I must wait in a line.
　　　C. I must wait at the information counter.
　　　D. I must wait in front of the ATM.

　　　* available (ə'veləbl) *adj.* 可獲得的；有空的　　tell ('tɛlɚ) *n.* 出納員
　　　information counter 服務台
　　　ATM 自動提款機 (= *automatic teller machine*)

For questions number 13 to 15, please look at picture H.

13. (**A**) Question number 13, what is "I" doing?
　　　A. He is raking leaves.
　　　B. He is driving a car.
　　　C. He is taking a walk.
　　　D. He is reading a newspaper.

　　　* rake (rek) *v.* 耙

14. (**C**) Question number 14, please look at picture H again. What is "D" doing?

    A. He is watching TV.

    B. He is making the bed.

    C. He is vacuuming.

    D. He is painting.

    * **make the bed** 舖床　　vacuum (ˈvækjʊm) v. 用吸塵器清掃

15. (**D**) Question number 15, please look at picture H again. What is "H" doing?

    A. He is carrying a trash can.

    B. He is making the bed.

    C. He is cleaning the house.

    D. He is watering the lawn and the plants.

    * water (ˈwɑtɚ) v. 澆水

Part B

16. (**D**) Does your father always eat at home?

    A. Yes, he sometimes eats at his friend's house.

    B. No, he always does.

    C. Yes, he sometimes eats at home.

    D. No, he sometimes eats at a restaurant.

17. (**C**) Why can't he leave tomorrow?

    A. I'm sorry to hear that.

    B. All right.

    C. Because he is very busy.

    D. No, he can't.

18. (**B**) How about going to the beach this weekend?

    A. You can take a city bus.

    B. That's a good idea.

    C. Give me a hand.

    D. That's too bad.

19. (**D**) What's the date?
　　A. It's summer.
　　B. It's Monday.
　　C. It's hot.
　　D. It's July 9.

20. (**B**) I like playing computer games more than seeing movies.
　　A. Do you like seeing movies?
　　B. So do I.
　　C. Neither do I.
　　D. I don't think so.

21. (**B**) I'll go mountain climbing this weekend with my family.
　　A. Don't give up now.
　　B. Have a good time.
　　C. No, I'm too tired.
　　D. I can't find it.
　　* *give up* 放棄

22. (**B**) Would you mind helping John carry this heavy box?
　　A. Certainly not.　I am glad to help you.
　　B. Of course not.　I am glad to.
　　C. Of course.　You are very kind.
　　D. No, he can carry it by himself.

23. (**C**) My sister put her old books on the highest shelf.
　　A. So am I.
　　B. So do I.
　　C. So did I.
　　D. So I was.

24. (**C**) Hurry up!　We will be late for school.
　　A. It's up to you.
　　B. Why not?
　　C. Take it easy.
　　D. That's a good idea.
　　* *Take it easy*! 放輕鬆！

25. (**D**) Hi, Mark.   Why do you look so tired today?
      A. That's too bad.
      B. I hope so.
      C. There's something special.
      D. I went to bed very late last night.

26. (**B**) Why do you look down?   Did something happen?
      A. I am looking down in order to look for my dog.
      B. I got bad grades in my tests yesterday.
      C. I have no idea why you look so sad.
      D. I am waiting for a bus.

      * down (daʊn) *adj.* 沮喪的

27. (**D**) What are the girls doing?
      A. They don't understand.
      B. They were in the living room.
      C. They don't like instant soup.
      D. They are swimming.

      * instant ('ɪnstənt) *adj.* 即溶的；速食的   soup (sup) *n.* 湯

28. (**D**) Will you and John play volleyball on the weekend?
      A. Not at all.   Thanks.
      B. I'd love to.
      C. What is it about?
      D. Yes, we will.

      * volleyball ('vɑlɪ,bɔl) *n.* 排球

29. (**D**) What's the matter?
      A. He works very hard.
      B. Young children like watching TV.
      C. That doesn't surprise me.
      D. There's something wrong with my bike.

30. (**A**) I forgot to mail the letter.
   A. Really?
   B. That's not bad.
   C. I don't know.
   D. You are all right.
   * mail (mel) *v.* 郵寄

Part C

31. (**A**) W: Here's my ticket. Where's my seat, please?
   M: The fourth row on the right, next to the window.
     We're going to be taking off shortly.

   (TONE)
   Q: Where is this conversation probably taking place?
   A. In an airplane.
   B. In a restaurant.
   C. In a stadium.
   D. In a movie theater.
   * row (ro) *n.* 排　　***take off*** 起飛
     shortly ('ʃɔrtlɪ) *adv.* 不久　　stadium ('stedɪəm) *n.* 體育館

32. (**D**) W: Steve looks good in that old jacket, doesn't he?
   M: I still wish he'd get a new one.

   (TONE)
   Q: What is the man's opinion?
   A. Steve looks good in anything.
   B. He knew someone who looked like Steve.
   C. He wishes he had a jacket like Steve.
   D. Steve should get a new jacket.

33. (**D**) W: I'm sorry, but I'm afraid you can't go in now. Mr. Smith is in a conference right now.

M: O.K. I'll just wait.

(TONE)

Q: Why can't the man see Mr. Smith?

A. Mr. Smith doesn't work there anymore.

B. Mr. Smith has too much work.

C. Mr. Smith is out of the building.

D. Mr. Smith is in a meeting.

* conference ('kɑnfərəns) *n.* 會議

34. (**D**) W: Good luck on your examination this afternoon.

M: I don't need good luck; I need another week to study for it.

(TONE)

Q: What does the man say about his examination?

A. It will be easy.

B. It was postponed.

C. He feels lucky.

D. He's not prepared.

* postpone (post'pon) *v.* 拖延;延期

35. (**C**) W: Shut the window. It's cold in here.

M: I'm just trying to let a little fresh air in.

(TONE)

Q: Why did the man open the window?

A. He was cold.

B. He was hot.

C. The air was stale.

D. The room was old.

* shut (ʃʌt) *v.* 關上   stale (stel) *adj.* 不新鮮的;有霉味的

36. (**B**) M: Have you seen my brother?

W: No, I haven't seen him since the day before yesterday.

(TONE)

Q: When did she last see the man's brother?

A. Yesterday.

B. Two days ago.

C. Three days ago.

D. Early last week.

* last (læst) *adv.* 上次

37. (**A**) M: Bill and I are giving a party this Friday night. Do you think you can make it?

W: Sure. Is it O.K. if I bring Barbara along, too?

(TONE)

Q: What does the man request?

A. That the woman come to the party.

B. A date with Barbara.

C. That the woman cook for the party.

D. A present for Bill.

* ***make it*** 成功；能來   request (rɪˈkwɛst) *v.* 要求

38. (**A**) M: Excuse me, could you please tell me how much this vase costs? I think I'd like to buy it.

W: I'm sorry but I don't work here.

(TONE)

Q: Why can't the woman answer the question?

A. She is also a customer.

B. The vase has already been sold.

C. She is new in town.

D. The vase is not for sale.

39. (**D**) W: I'd like to get a babysitter for this Saturday night. Can you
   recommend anyone?
   M: My son's girlfriend seems to be responsible, trustworthy,
   and she likes children.

   (TONE)

   Q: What does the man think the woman should do?
   A. She should find someone who likes children.
   B. She should hire someone responsible and trustworthy.
   C. She should hire his son.
   D. She should hire his son's girlfriend.

   * babysitter ('bebɪ,sɪtə) *n.* 褓姆　　recommend (,rɛkə'mɛnd) *v.* 推薦
   trustworthy ('trʌst,wɜðɪ) *adj.* 值得信賴的

40. (**B**) M: If you'd like, I can ask the waitress to bring you another
   piece of apple pie.
   W: Oh, no, thank you. I've already eaten so much, I couldn't
   eat another bite. The food here is really something.

   (TONE)

   Q: Where did the conversation most probably take place?
   A. At a buffet.
   B. At a restaurant.
   C. At someone's house.
   D. At a dinner party.

   * bite (baɪt) *n.* 一口　　something ('sʌmθɪŋ) *n.* 了不起的東西
   buffet (bʊ'fe) *n.* (歐式) 自助餐

41. (**B**) W: Richard spent his summer in Alaska, didn't he?
   M: I wouldn't know; I haven't seen him for months.

   (TONE)

   Q: What doesn't the man know?
   A. How Richard traveled.
   B. Where Richard went.
   C. If Richard will go.
   D. How much Richard spent.

42. (**A**) M: If the traffic wasn't so bad, I could have been home by 6:00.

W: It's too bad you didn't get here. Jack was here and he wanted to see you.

(TONE)

Q: What happened to the man?

A. He was held up in traffic.

B. He had no way to get home.

C. He was busy at the office.

D. His car had to be repaired.

* ***hold up*** 使耽擱　　repair (rɪ'pɛr) *v.* 修理

43. (**D**) M: The air conditioner in my room is broken and I can't work.

W: Why not go to the library?

(TONE)

Q: What does the woman mean?

A. The man can find work in the library.

B. She can't help the man because she's working.

C. She can work without air conditioning.

D. The man can do his work elsewhere.

* ***air conditioner*** 冷氣機　　broken ('brokən) *adj.* 故障的

elsewhere ('ɛls,hwɛr) *adv.* 在別處

44. (**D**) M: Our team won yesterday's volleyball game.

W: Oh, you're getting better, aren't you?

(TONE)

Q: What does the woman mean?

A. The team played one hour longer yesterday.

B. The team had better play one more game.

C. The man should join a better team.

D. The man's team is improving.

* team (tim) *n.* 隊　　improve (ɪm'pruv) *v.* 改進

45. (**A**) W: Stanley looks thinner. Is he on a diet?

M: No, he just knows how to dress so as to make himself look thinner.

(TONE)

Q: Why does the woman think that Stanley might be on a diet?

A. He looks like he's lost weight.

B. He exercises regularly.

C. He doesn't eat much.

D. He told her so.

* thin (θɪn) *adj.* 瘦的　　***be on a diet*** 節食

　 regularly ('rɛgjələlɪ) *adv.* 定期地

Part D

46. (**B**) Thank you for calling the Rax Theater. This week's feature is "The Man Without a Face," starring Tim Smith and Laura Lee. Daily show times are at 2:00 p.m. and 7:00 p.m.

(TONE)

Q: How many times a day is the show given?

A. Once.

B. Twice.

C. Three times.

D. Four times.

* feature ('fitʃɚ) *n.* 電影長片　　star (stɑr) *v.* 由～主演

47. (**C**) Every day this week, the works of Picasso's Blue Period will be shown in the video viewing room, which is located on the third floor. The showing is from 3:00 p.m. to 4:00 p.m. Admission is free.

(TONE)

Q: Where is the viewing room?

A. In the lobby.

B. In the basement.

C. On the 3rd floor.

D. On the 4th floor.

　*　*be located on* 位於　admission (əd'mıʃən) *n.* 入場費
　basement ('besmənt) *n.* 地下室

48. (**C**) Attention passengers.　Our landing has been delayed due to the overcrowded condition of Kennedy Airport.　As the situation at Kennedy may not improve, we have decided to land at the nearest local airport.　Landing will be in 25 minutes.

(TONE)

Q: Where can this announcement be heard?

A. On the bus.

B. At an airport.

C. On the plane.

D. In front of a boarding gate.

　*　landing ('lændıŋ) *n.* 降落　delay (dı'le) *v.* 延誤
　announcement (ə'naʊnsmənt) *n.* 宣布　*boarding gate* 登機門

49. (**A**) This is a recording.　You have reached the Northeast Medical Information Center.　We are sorry that we have already closed for the day.　You can leave your name, phone number, and a message concerning your medical condition, or call us back tomorrow if you wish to talk to us directly.　All medical advisers are available from 11 to 4, Tuesday through Friday. Thank you for calling.

(TONE)

Q: Who can the caller talk to directly?

A. Advisers.

B. Medical operators.

C. Travel agents.

D. Doctors.

* adviser (əd'vaɪsə) *n.* 顧問　　through (θru) *prep.* 直到
operator ('ɑpə,retə) *n.* 動手術的人　　agent ('edʒənt) *n.* 代理人

50. (**D**) You are listening to the Voice of Washington State.　This is
WXYW, the Pacific Ocean station.　The news at noon has been
brought to you by Citizen's Bank.

(TONE)

Q: Who sponsored the news broadcast?

A. Washington State.

B. The Pacific Ocean station.

C. WXYW.

D. Citizen's Bank.

* sponsor ('spɑnsə) *v.* 贊助　　broadcast ('brɔd,kæst) *v.* 廣播

51. (**C**) May I have your attention, please?　At this moment I would
like to introduce Mr. Michael Jameson, who was formerly a
director in our advertising division prior to his present career as
a professor at the University of California.

(TONE)

Q: What position does Mr. Jameson currently hold?

A. Vice-president of the company.

B. Director of the advertising division.

C. Professor at a university.

D. Manager of the company.

* formerly ('fɔrməlɪ) *adv.* 以前　　director (də'rɛktə) *n.* 主任
division (də'vɪʒən) *n.* 部門　　currently ('kɝəntlɪ) *adv.* 目前
prior to 在～之前

52. (**C**) The islanders were short, strong people, with a very well-organized social system. The men fished and raised crops including taro, coconuts, sweet potatoes, and sugar cane. The women cared for the children and made clothing that consisted of loin-cloths for the men and short skirts for the women.

(TONE)
Q: What did the native women do?
A. They fished and raised crops.
B. They cared for the children and raised crops.
C. They cared for the children and made clothing.
D. They made clothing and raised animals.

   * islander (ˈaɪləndɚ) *n.* 島上居民   raise (rez) *v.* 種植
   taro (ˈtɑro) *n.* 芋頭   loin-cloth (ˈlɔɪnˌklθ) *n.* 腰布
   native (ˈnetɪv) *adj.* 當地的

53. (**D**) Rain didn't stop them from doing their job. Nor did snow, ice, fog, or even the extreme heat of the sun. Even typhoons couldn't slow down their pace of work.

(TONE)
Q: What does the passage imply?
A. They worked in sun and rain.
B. They worked all the year round.
C. They went out to work even in typhoons.
D. They worked in all weathers.

   * pace (pes) *n.* 步調   ***all the year round*** 全年

54. (**B**) We have a forty percent chance of snow this afternoon, and a twenty percent chance tomorrow. At one o'clock our current temperature is thirty degrees.

(TONE)

Q: What time was this weather forecast reported?

A. Ten o'clock.

B. One o'clock.

C. One-thirty.

D. Two o'clock.

* current ('kɜənt) *adj.* 目前的

55. (**B**) Samuel F.B. Morse invented a successful telegraph and obtained a patent on it in 1841. He wanted the federal government to develop a telegraph system; however, Congress refused to provide money for this purpose. That's why the telegraph network became a private industry.

(TONE)

Q: How did Congress feel about developing a telegraph system?

A. Congress was willing to develop a telegraph system.

B. Congress refused to appropriate money for the purpose.

C. Congress assisted private corporations to develop the telegraph system.

D. Congress believed the telegraph system was worthless.

* telegraph ('tɛlə,græf) *n.* 電報　　patent ('petṇt) *n.* 專利
federal ('fɛdərəl) *adj.* 聯邦的　　Congress ('kɑŋgrɛs) *n.* 國會
network ('nɛt,wɜk) *n.* 網路　　appropriate (ə'proprɪ,et) *v.* 撥 (款)
corporation (,kɔrpə'reʃən) *n.* 公司

56. (**D**) Before 1800, only a few well-known institutions — Harvard, Yale, and Princeton — which had been established by religious groups, offered the opportunity for a college education. Their purpose was to train ministers.

(TONE)

Q: What did college education, before 1800, imply?

A. Raising funds.

B. Lifting the nation's cultural level.

C. Establishing free schools.

D. Training ministers.

* minister ('mɪnɪstɚ) *n.* 牧師　　raise (rez) *v.* 籌募
　fund (fʌnd) *n.* 基金　　level ('lɛvḷ) *n.* 水準

57. (**C**) Tree borers are serious business wherever they appear. They can, and often do, destroy beautiful trees regardless of age or species. Tree borers promise to be especially troublesome this year. Last summer's heat and prolonged drought weakened many trees. Once a tree is weakened, they seem to be attracted to it.

(TONE)

Q: Last summer what made trees weaken?

A. Lack of nutrients.　　　　B. Snow and ice.

C. Heat and drought.　　　　D. Old age.

* borer ('borɚ) *n.* 鑽木頭的蟲　　species ('spiʃɪz) *n.* 種
　promise ('prɑmɪs) *v.* 有可能　　prolonged (prə'lɔŋd) *adj.* 長期的
　drought (draʊt) *n.* 乾旱　　nutrient ('njutrɪənt) *n.* 營養素

58. (**B**) Looking for a truly rewarding investment? Are you dissatisfied with routine analysis of the market? The financial magazine "Economic Time", which has been the leader of its kind for over 50 years, is now offering you a great opportunity for innovative strategy.

(TONE)

Q: With what is "Economic Time" primarily concerned?

A. Business leadership.　　　B. Investment.

C. History.　　　　　　　　D. Seminar.

* rewarding (rɪ'wɔrdɪŋ) *adj.* 獲利的　　routine (ru'tin) *adj.* 一般的
　innovative ('ɪno,vetɪv) *adj.* 革新的　　strategy ('strætədʒɪ) *n.* 策略
　primarily ('praɪmɛrəlɪ) *adv.* 主要地　　seminar ('sɛmə,nɑr) *n.* 研討會

59. (**C**) I'd like to tell you about an interesting TV program that'll be shown this coming Thursday. It'll be on from 9 to 10 p.m. on Channel 4. It's part of a series called "Mysteries of Human Biology." The subject of the program is the human brain — how it functions and how it can malfunction.

(TONE)

Q: What is the main purpose of the program?

A. To demonstrate the latest use of computer graphics.

B. To discuss the possibility of an economic depression.

C. To explain the workings of the brain.

D. To dramatize a famous mystery story.

* series ('sɪrɪz) *n.* 電視系列片　malfunction (ˌmæl'fʌŋkʃən) *n.* 機能失常
demonstrate ('dɛmən͵stret) *v.* 示範　graphics ('græfɪks) *n.* 繪圖法
dramatize ('dræmə͵taɪz) *v.* 把~編爲戲劇　*mystery story* 推理小說

60. (**C**) Police have ticketed more than 2,200 drivers in a crackdown on speeding in the past four weeks. But officers said drivers are not slowing down. "We've still got 70 percent-plus non-compliance with the speed limit," said officer Chipman, who is directing the crackdown.

(TONE)

Q: What is Chipman?

A. A driver who got a speeding ticket.

B. A newspaper editor who wrote this article.

C. An officer who is directing the crackdown.

D. A visitor who is traveling.

* crackdown ('kræk͵daʊn) *n.* 取締
non-compliance (ˌnɑnkəm'plaɪəns) *n.* 不遵守

English Listening Comprehension Test

Test Book No. 4

This listening comprehension test will test your ability to understand spoken English. In this test, each conversation, statement and question will be spoken JUST ONE TIME. They will not be written out for you. There are four parts to this test. Special instructions will be given to you at the beginning of each part.

Part A

In Part A, you will see several pictures in your test book. For each picture, you will be asked 1 to 3 questions. For each question, you will hear four possible answers. Choose the best answer according to what you see in the picture.

Example:

You will see:

You will hear: What is this?
A. This is a table.
B. This is a chair.
C. This is a watch.
D. This is a doll.

The best answer to the question "What is this?" is B: "This is a chair." Therefore, you should choose answer B.

A. Questions 1-3

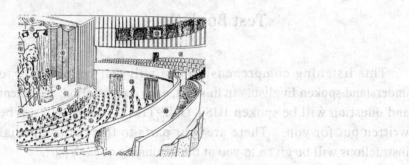

B. Questions 4-6   ## C. Questions 7-8

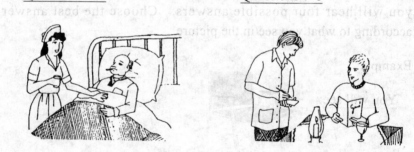

D. Question 9

E. Questions 10-12

F. Questions 13-15

Part B

In Part B, you will hear 15 questions. After you hear a question, read the four possible answers in your test book and decide which one is the best answer to the question you have heard.

Example:

<u>You will hear:</u>   What does your father do?

<u>You will read:</u>   A. He's 50 years old.
　　　　　　　　　B. He's a teacher.
　　　　　　　　　C. He's hungry.
　　　　　　　　　D. He's in Los Angeles.

The best answer to the question "What does your father do?" is B: "He's a teacher." Therefore, you should choose answer B.

Please go to the next page. ⟹

16. A. Yes, thank you.
    B. It is 5 dollars.
    C. We don't have any homework.
    D. I hope so.

17. A. Are you here?
    B. Let's go home.
    C. It always is.
    D. I stop it.

18. A. He doesn't run every day.
    B. He runs fast every day.
    C. He is too old to run.
    D. As fast as you.

19. A. His brother is, too.
    B. Neither does his brother.
    C. So is his brother.
    D. So does his brother.

20. A. It's very warm in winter.
    B. The weather is nice in winter.
    C. It's too cold in winter.
    D. No, they don't take a trip every winter.

21. A. How are you? Nice to see you again.
    B. Thank you. Glad to see you.
    C. How do you do? Nice to meet you.
    D. Have you eaten breakfast?

22. A. I bought a new car.
    B. By bus.
    C. I rode a bicycle.
    D. By studying.

23. A. Parking is never easy.
    B. There's no parking along this street.
    C. Look! Every car is gone!
    D. Because they liked to.

24. A. By car.
    B. Very quick.
    C. To Taipei.
    D. In a few minutes.

25. A. It must be Kevin.
    B. I would like to stay at home.
    C. I am so surprised.
    D. It doesn't interest me.

26. A. I'm interested in math.
　　B. English is really an easy subject.
　　C. I become excited about Chinese.
　　D. I can't find a satisfying answer.

27. A. It won't write.
　　B. Yes, I have a good pen.
　　C. I don't need it.
　　D. This is a new pen.

28. A. On Monday.
　　B. It's Saturday.
　　C. On Tuesday and Thursday.
　　D. On Sunday morning.

29. A. Oh, that's too bad!
　　B. Yes, it is.
　　C. Have a good time!
　　D. Of course, they can.

30. A. It's too hot in winter.
　　B. I love it.
　　C. So far so good.
　　D. That's all right.

Part C

In Part C, you will hear 15 conversations between a man and a woman. After each conversation, you will hear a question about the conversation.   After you hear the question, read the four possible answers in your test book and choose the best answer to the question you have heard.

Example:

You will hear: (Man)   How do you go to school every day?
                 (Woman)   Usually by bus.   Sometimes by taxi.

                 TONE: How does the woman go to school?

You will read: A. She always goes to school on foot.
                 B. She usually takes a bike.
                 C. She takes either a bus or a taxi.
                 D. She usually goes to school by bus, never by
                     taxi.

The best answer to the question "How does the woman go to school?" is C: "She takes either a bus or a taxi."   Therefore, you should choose answer C.

Please go to the next page. ⇨

31. A. He always eats more than
     he can.
    B. He eats while studying and
     working.
    C. He got sick because he ate
     too much.
    D. He is trying to study and
     work too much.

32. A. His tonsils are swollen.
    B. He doesn't feel well because
     he drank too much.
    C. He has trouble breathing
     after jogging.
    D. He has no appetite because
     he caught a cold.

33. A. At a zoo.
    B. At a museum.
    C. In a college cafeteria.
    D. At a bird house.

34. A. He is impudent.
    B. He is courageous.
    C. He is nervous.
    D. He is intelligent.

35. A. Because something was
     wrong with the lights.
    B. Because the electricity failed.
    C. Because the engineer made
     an error.
    D. Because the woman hadn't
     paid the electric bills for
     months.

36. A. Went to see the movie.
    B. Fell asleep.
    C. Played football.
    D. Watched the late movie.

37. A. He spilled coffee and
     discolored his shirt.
    B. He broke a coffee cup.
    C. He can't find an
     encyclopedia.
    D. He discolored the shirt
     with dirt.

38. A. The number of the
     publication.
    B. The name of the
     bookstore.
    C. The title of the book
     which will be most
     popular.
    D. The publisher's name.

39. A. It is too late for the
     woman to get a ticket.
    B. The woman must change
     her destination.
    C. The woman should wait
     until tomorrow.
    D. She will never be able to
     get a ticket.

40. A. The man must have been
    mistaken.
   B. It has been a long time
    since she went to see the
    show.
   C. Peter couldn't have been
    that old.
   D. Peter must be old because
    it has been years since
    she saw him.

41. A. Type the report.
   B. Write a report.
   C. Type the proposals.
   D. Attend the meeting.

42. A. Writing a research paper
    is a pain for her.
   B. She has a class at three
    o'clock.
   C. She hopes that she doesn't
    have to write a paper.
   D. She doesn't want to
    trouble him.

43. A. She can get two dresses and
    a pair of socks for 24 dollars.
   B. She shouldn't buy the dress
    because it's not a bargain.
   C. She can have free socks if
    she pays him 12 dollars for
    the dress.
   D. She will earn twelve dollars
    by selling socks.

44. A. He will take a sports class.
   B. He will pick up jogging.
   C. He will pursue athletics.
   D. He will go for his athletics
    teacher.

45. A. The restaurant was entirely
    destroyed by fire.
   B. The restaurant was open
    last July.
   C. The restaurant went bankrupt.
   D. The restaurant has been in
    the black since July.

Part D

In Part D, you will hear 15 short talks. After each talk, you will hear a question about the talk. After you hear the question, read the four possible answers in your test book and choose the best answer to the question you have heard.

Example:

You will hear: Well, that's all for Unit 15. For today's homework, please do the review questions on page 80, and we'll check the answers tomorrow. Now, let's go on to Unit 16.

TONE: What is the teacher going to do next in today's class?

You will read: A. Check the homework.
B. Review Unit 15.
C. Start a new unit.
D. Answer students' questions.

The best answer to the question "What is the teacher going to do next in today's class?" is C: "Start a new unit." Therefore, you should choose answer C.

Please go to the next page. ⇨

46. A. Learned to do paper sculpture.
    B. Designed and built houses.
    C. Worked on drawing house plans.
    D. Given talks about famous architects.

47. A. Humorous.
    B. Tragic.
    C. Sad.
    D. Dark.

48. A. At the main entrance.
    B. In the gift shop.
    C. From the shopkeeper.
    D. At the primate center.

49. A. The treatment of burns.
    B. The process of conscious thought.
    C. The body's ability to heal itself.
    D. The body's unconscious reactions.

50. A. Basketball.
    B. Soccer.
    C. Table tennis.
    D. Baseball.

51. A. He went rabbit hunting.
    B. He was attacked by a rabbit.
    C. He went fishing.
    D. He went jogging.

52. A. Learning English.
    B. Learning conversation skills.
    C. Learning about foreign places.
    D. Learning a foreign language.

53. A. Cowboys.
    B. Frontiersmen.
    C. Indians.
    D. Film makers.

54. A. On a bus.
    B. In a taxi.
    C. On an airplane.
    D. On the mass rapid transit system.

55. A. A customer.
    B. A boss.
    C. A teacher.
    D. An operator.

56. A. A TV sports announcer.
    B. A bike salesman.
    C. A facility manager.
    D. A teacher.

57. A. Soup.
    B. Beer.
    C. Bread.
    D. Soft drink.

58. A. At a history lecture.
    B. At a company which buys insurance.
    C. At a meeting of employees.
    D. At a birthday party.

59. A. A trip to Taipei.
    B. The number of employees.
    C. The name of a restaurant.
    D. The charges of rooms.

60. A. The woman's wealth.
    B. A note from a church.
    C. Where the woman lived.
    D. The woman's age.

Listening Test 4 詳解

Part A

For questions number 1 to 3, please look at picture A.

1. (**C**) Question number 1, what is this a typical picture of?
   A. This is a cinema.
   B. This is a lecture hall.
   C. This is a theater.
   D. This is an orchestra.

   * cinema ('sɪnəmə) *n.* 電影院　　*lecture hall* 演講廳
   theater ('θiətə) *n.* 戲劇院　　orchestra ('ɔrkɪstrə) *n.* 管絃樂團

2. (**B**) Question number 2, please look at picture A again.　Where are the actors standing?
   A. They are standing on a stair.
   B. They are standing on a stage.
   C. They are standing on a screen.
   D. They are standing on a building.

   * stair (stɛr) *n.* 階梯　　stage (stedʒ) *n.* 舞台　　screen (skrin) *n.* 螢幕

3. (**C**) Question number 3, please look at picture A again.　Is the show popular?
   A. Yes, it is sold out.
   B. Yes, there is standing room only.
   C. No, it is not very popular.
   D. We can't tell from the picture.

   * *standing room only* 只剩站位

For questions number 4 to 6, please look at picture B.

4. (**B**) Question number 4, what is the woman?
   A. She is a doctor.
   B. She is a nurse.
   C. She is a patient.
   D. She is a waiter.

5. (**C**) Question number 5, please look at picture B again. What's the woman doing?

    A. She is taking the man's weight and temperature.

    B. She is taking the man's blood pressure.

    C. She is taking the man's temperature and pulse.

    D. She is taking the man's pulse and weight.

    * pulse (pʌls) *n.* 脈搏

6. (**A**) Question number 6, please look at picture B again. What does the man have in his mouth?

    A. The man has a thermometer in his mouth.

    B. The man has a glass in his mouth.

    C. The man has a needle in his mouth.

    D. The man has a stethoscope in his mouth.

    * thermometer (θəˈmɑmətɚ) *n.* 溫度計

    stethoscope (ˈstɛθəˌskop) *n.* 聽診器

For questions number 7 to 8, please look at picture C.

7. (**D**) Question number 7, what is the customer doing?

    A. The customer is paying his bill.

    B. The customer is eating.

    C. The customer is reading.

    D. The customer is ordering food.

8. (**C**) Question number 8, please look at picture C again. What is on the table?

    A. There is a lamp on the table.

    B. There is a book on the table.

    C. There is a candle on the table.

    D. There is a plate on the table.

    * plate (plet) *n.* 大的淺盤

For question number 9, please look at picture D.

9. (**C**) Question number 9, what are the men doing?
    A. The men are playing a game.
    B. The men are fighting.
    C. The men are shaking hands.
    D. The men are sitting.

For questions number 10 to 12, please look at picture E.

10. (**B**) Question number 10, where are they?
    A. They are in a hospital.
    B. They are in a restaurant.
    C. They are in a railroad station.
    D. They are in a hotel lobby.
    * lobby ('lɑbɪ) *n.* （旅館）大廳

11. (**C**) Question number 11, please look at picture E again.　What is the waiter holding?
    A. He is holding a glass.
    B. He is holding a flower.
    C. He is holding a pizza.
    D. He is holding a menu.

12. (**B**) Question number 12, please look at picture E again.　What is the waiter wearing?
    A. The waiter is wearing glasses.
    B. The waiter is wearing a bow tie.
    C. The waiter is wearing a mustache.
    D. The waiter is wearing a scarf.
    * ***bow tie*** 領結；蝴蝶結
    mustache ('mʌstæʃ , mə'stæʃ) *n.* （嘴唇上的）髭

For questions number 13 to 15, please look at picture F.

13. (**B**) Question number 13, what is the man doing?

    A. He is taking a bath.

    B. He is opening the medicine cabinet.

    C. He is washing his hands.

    D. He is doing the dishes.

    * cabinet (ˈkæbənɪt) *n.* (有玻璃門的) 櫥櫃

14. (**A**) Question number 14, please look at picture F again.　What is to the left of the sink?

    A. It is a trash can.

    B. It is a clothes hamper.

    C. It is a toilet.

    D. It is a toilet paper holder.

    * *to the left of* 在～的左邊　　hamper (ˈhæmpɚ) *n.* 洗衣籃
    toilet (ˈtɔɪlɪt) *n.* 馬桶　　*toilet paper holder* 衛生紙置放架

15. (**B**) Question number 15, please look at picture F again.　What is number "11"?

    A. It is a sink.

    B. It is a towel.

    C. It is a bathtub.

    D. It is a shower curtain.

    * curtain (ˈkɝtn̩) *n.* 簾子　　*shower curtain* 浴簾

Part B

16. (**C**) How much homework do you have?

    A. Yes, thank you.

    B. It is 5 dollars.

    C. We don't have any homework.

    D. I hope so.

17. (**B**) It is getting late.
　　　　A. Are you here?
　　　　B. Let's go home.
　　　　C. It always is.
　　　　D. I stop it.

18. (**D**) How fast does Bob run?
　　　　A. He doesn't run every day.
　　　　B. He runs fast every day.
　　　　C. He is too old to run.
　　　　D. As fast as you.

19. (**D**) Mr. Wang owns a bookstore.
　　　　A. His brother is, too.
　　　　B. Neither does his brother.
　　　　C. So is his brother.
　　　　D. So does his brother.

20. (**C**) Why don't they take a trip in winter?
　　　　A. It's very warm in winter.
　　　　B. The weather is nice in winter.
　　　　C. It's too cold in winter.
　　　　D. No, they don't take a trip every winter.

21. (**C**) Tom, this is Jack, and Jack, this is Tom.
　　　　A. How are you?　Nice to see you again.
　　　　B. Thank you.　Glad to see you.
　　　　C. How do you do?　Nice to meet you.
　　　　D. Have you eaten breakfast?

22. (**B**) How do you go to school every day?
　　　　A. I bought a new car.
　　　　B. By bus.
　　　　C. I rode a bicycle.
　　　　D. By studying.

23. (**B**) Why did the police take all the cars away?
      A. Parking is never easy.
      B. There's no parking along this street.
      C. Look! Every car is gone!
      D. Because they liked to.

24. (**D**) How soon will he come back home?
      A. By car.
      B. Very quick.
      C. To Taipei.
      D. In a few minutes.

25. (**A**) The door bell is ringing. Would you see who it is?
      A. It must be Kevin.
      B. I would like to stay at home.
      C. I am so surprised.
      D. It doesn't interest me.

26. (**D**) Why do you look so confused?
      A. I'm interested in math.
      B. English is really an easy subject.
      C. I become excited about Chinese.
      D. I can't find a satisfying answer.

27. (**A**) Is there anything wrong with your pen?
      A. It won't write.
      B. Yes, I have a good pen.
      C. I don't need it.
      D. This is a new pen.

28. (**C**) What days does Joe study English?
      A. On Monday.
      B. It's Saturday.
      C. On Tuesday and Thursday.
      D. On Sunday morning.

29. (**C**) I'm going to have a picnic tomorrow.
    A. Oh, that's too bad!   B. Yes, it is.
    C. Have a good time!   D. Of course, they can.

30. (**B**) How do you feel about the fall, Helen?
    A. It's too hot in winter.   B. I love it.
    C. So far so good.   D. That's all right.

Part C

31. (**D**) M: Did you hear that Bob got sick yesterday during the final
      examination?
    W: Yes, I did. I think lately he has bitten off more than he can
      chew in studying and working.

   (TONE)
   Q: What does the woman mean?
   A. He always eats more than he can.
   B. He eats while studying and working.
   C. He got sick because he ate too much.
   D. He is trying to study and work too much.
   * bite off more than one can chew* 貪多嚼不爛；事情太多做不完

32. (**B**) W: What's the matter with you today?
    M: Oh boy. I've got a terrible hangover.

   (TONE)
   Q: What's the man's problem?
   A. His tonsils are swollen.
   B. He doesn't feel well because he drank too much.
   C. He has trouble breathing after jogging.
   D. He has no appetite because he caught a cold.
   * hangover* (ˈhæŋˌovɚ) *n.* 宿醉   tonsil (ˈtɑnsḷ) *n.* 扁桃腺
   swollen (ˈswolən) *adj.* 腫的   appetite (ˈæpəˌtaɪt) *n.* 食慾

33. (**A**) M: Where would you like to go next?

W: I really would like to see the reptiles but let's go to see the peacocks, since it's 12 o'clock. It's the best time to see them spreading their wings.

(TONE)

Q: Where are these people?

A. At a zoo.

B. At a museum.

C. In a college cafeteria.

D. At a bird house.

* reptile (ˈrɛptḷ) *n.* 爬蟲類　　peacock (ˈpiˌkɑk) *n.* 孔雀
cafeteria (ˌkæfəˈtɪrɪə) *n.* 自助餐廳

34. (**A**) W: Why are you so provoked?

M: I had to study for tomorrow's biology test but Robert had the nerve to listen to the stereo for two hours.

(TONE)

Q: What does the man mean about Robert?

A. He is impudent.

B. He is courageous.

C. He is nervous.

D. He is intelligent.

* provoked (prəˈvokt) *adj.* 生氣的　　*have the nerve to-V* 厚顏做~
impudent (ˈɪmpjədənt) *adj.* 無恥的
courageous (kəˈredʒəs) *adj.* 勇敢的

35. (**C**) W: I wonder why the electricity went out this morning.

M: It happened because of an oversight on the part of the engineer.

(TONE)

Q: Why did the electricity go out?

A. Because something was wrong with the lights.

B. Because the electricity failed.

C. Because the engineer made an error.

D. Because the woman hadn't paid the electric bills for months.

* **go out** 熄滅　　oversight ('ovɚ,saɪt) n. 疏忽
  on the part of 在～方面　　bill (bɪl) n. 帳單

36. (**B**) W: Did you see the late movie on TV last night?

M: No, I intended to watch the football game but slept through it.

(TONE)

Q: What did the man do last night?

A. Went to see the movie.

B. Fell asleep.

C. Played football.

D. Watched the late movie.

37. (**A**) M: Barbara, how can I remove coffee stains on my shirt?

W: I don't know.　Why don't you check an encyclopedia?

(TONE)

Q: What's the man's problem?

A. He spilled coffee and discolored his shirt.

B. He broke a coffee cup.

C. He can't find an encyclopedia.

D. He discolored the shirt with dirt.

* remove (rɪ'muv) v. 除去　　stain (sten) n. 污漬
  encyclopedia (ɪn,saɪklə'pidɪə) n. 百科全書
  spill (spɪl) v. 灑；潑
  discolored (dɪs'kʌlɚ) v. 使變色；褪色

38. (**C**) M: Which book will sell the most copies?
　　　　 W: I am afraid I have no idea which book will sell.

　　　　 (TONE)
　　　　 Q: What is the man asking about?
　　　　 A. The number of the publication.
　　　　 B. The name of the bookstore.
　　　　 C. The title of the book which will be most popular.
　　　　 D. The publisher's name.

　　　　 * publication (ˌpʌblɪˈkeʃən) n. 出版；發行
　　　　　 title (ˈtaɪtḷ) n. 書名　　publisher (ˈpʌblɪʃə) n. 出版社

39. (**A**) W: I'd like to fly to Los Angeles at 3 o'clock this afternoon.
　　　　　　 Do you have a one way ticket to LA?
　　　　 M: No seats at all to LA this afternoon.　All you can do is go
　　　　　　 stand by.

　　　　 (TONE)
　　　　 Q: What does the man mean?
　　　　 A. It is too late for the woman to get a ticket.
　　　　 B. The woman must change her destination.
　　　　 C. The woman should wait until tomorrow.
　　　　 D. She will never be able to get a ticket.

　　　　 * *one way ticket* 單程票　　*stand by* 候補
　　　　　 destination (ˌdɛstəˈneʃən) n. 目的地

40. (**A**) M: I thought it was Peter who was with you yesterday.
　　　　 W: That couldn't have been Peter because I haven't seen him
　　　　　　 for ages.

　　　　 (TONE)
　　　　 Q: What does the woman mean?
　　　　 A. The man must have been mistaken.
　　　　 B. It has been a long time since she went to see the show.
　　　　 C. Peter couldn't have been that old.
　　　　 D. Peter must be old because it has been years since she saw him.

　　　　 * *for ages* 很久

41. (**A**) W: Was I supposed to type this report this week?

　　　　 M: No, I assigned it to Mary.　Why don't you type these proposals for the meeting next week?

　　　　 (TONE)

　　　　 Q: What is Mary going to do this week?

　　　　 A. Type the report.

　　　　 B. Write a report.

　　　　 C. Type the proposals.

　　　　 D. Attend the meeting.

　　　　 * ***be supposed to*** 應該　　assign (ə'saɪn) v. 指派
　　　　 proposal (prə'pozḷ) n. 提議；計劃書

42. (**D**) M: If you want to talk about a topic for your term paper, why don't you come back at 3 this afternoon?

　　　　 W: Thank you.　I hope my request isn't inconvenient for you.

　　　　 (TONE)

　　　　 Q: What does the woman mean?

　　　　 A. Writing a research paper is a pain for her.

　　　　 B. She has a class at three o'clock.

　　　　 C. She hopes that she doesn't have to write a paper.

　　　　 D. She doesn't want to trouble him.

　　　　 * request (rɪ'kwɛst) n. 要求

43. (**C**) W: I think this dress is too expensive.

　　　　 M: You can have it for 12 dollars with a pair of socks thrown in.

　　　　 (TONE)

　　　　 Q: What does the man mean?

　　　　 A. She can get two dresses and a pair of socks for 24 dollars.

　　　　 B. She shouldn't buy the dress because it's not a bargain.

　　　　 C. She can have free socks if she pays him 12 dollars for the dress.

　　　　 D. She will earn twelve dollars by selling socks.

　　　　 * ***throw in*** 贈送　　bargain ('bɑrgɪn) n. 便宜的東西

44. (**C**) W: What are you going to do after graduating from college?
　　　　　 M: I guess I'll take up athletics seriously.

　　　　　 (TONE)
　　　　　 Q: What does the man mean?
　　　　　 A. He will take a sports class.
　　　　　 B. He will pick up jogging.
　　　　　 C. He will pursue athletics.
　　　　　 D. He will go for his athletics teacher.
　　　　　 * *take up* 開始學　　athletics (æθ'lɛtɪks) *n.* 體育（學科）
　　　　　 pursue (pɚ'su) *v.* 追求　　*go for* 喜歡

45. (**A**) W: Where's that Italian restaurant that used to be here?
　　　　　 M: It burned to the ground last July.

　　　　　 (TONE)
　　　　　 Q: What does the man mean?
　　　　　 A. The restaurant was entirely destroyed by fire.
　　　　　 B. The restaurant was open last July.
　　　　　 C. The restaurant went bankrupt.
　　　　　 D. The restaurant has been in the black since July.
　　　　　 * *burn to the ground* 燒毀　　*go bankrupt* 破產　　*in the black* 有盈餘

Part D

46. (**C**) Now that you've put some time into the practical work of this
　　　　　 course, drawing house plans, let's go back to our continuing
　　　　　 discussion of famous architects.

　　　　　 (TONE)
　　　　　 Q: What had the students done before this lecture?
　　　　　 A. Learned to do paper sculpture.
　　　　　 B. Designed and built houses.
　　　　　 C. Worked on drawing house plans.
　　　　　 D. Given talks about famous architects.
　　　　　 * architect ('ɑrkə,tɛkt) *n.* 建築師　　sculpture ('skʌlptʃɚ) *n.* 雕刻

47. (**A**) *To Be or Not to Be*? is a humorous film about England's greatest poet and playwright, William Shakespeare. It's the story of Shakespeare's life, and, though it's mostly a comedy, the film does probe into more serious questions about the origins of the plays Shakespeare is said to have written.

(TONE)
Q: How could this film best be described?
A. Humorous.
B. Tragic.
C. Sad.
D. Dark.

* humorous ('hjumərəs) *adj.* 幽默的　playwright ('pleˌraɪt) *n.* 劇作家
comedy ('kɑmədɪ) *n.* 喜劇　***probe into*** 探索
tragic ('trædʒɪk) *adj.* 悲慘的

48. (**A**) If you have any questions about these shows or other upcoming events at the zoo, please ask at the information booth at the main entrance next to the gift shop. Thank you.

(TONE)
Q: Where does the announcer say that a person can get information about the shows?
A. At the main entrance.
B. In the gift shop.
C. From the shopkeeper.
D. At the primate center.

* upcoming ('ʌpˌkʌmɪŋ) *adj.* 即將到來的　booth (buθ) *n.* 台
announcer (ə'naʊnsɚ) *n.* 廣播者；播音員
primate ('praɪmet) *n.* 靈長類動物

49. (**D**) If you accidentally touch a hot stove, you jerk your hand away before you're badly burned. If you had to think before acting, you might be severely hurt. This ability to act quickly and without conscious thought is called a reflex.

(TONE)

Q: What is the main topic of this talk?

A. The treatment of burns.

B. The process of conscious thought.

C. The body's ability to heal itself.

D. The body's unconscious reactions.

* jerk (dʒɜk) v. 猛然一拉　severely (sə'vɪrlɪ) adv. 嚴重地
  conscious ('kɑnʃəs) adj. 有意識的　reflex ('riflɛks) n. 反射動作

50. (**B**) An interesting Mayan structure is the Temple of the Tigers.
Nearby is a ball court, used for a game resembling soccer.
To lose was fatal: the losing captain was decapitated and his
wife taken as concubine by the victor.

(TONE)

Q: What modern sport did the outdoor game of the Mayans
resemble?

A. Basketball.

B. Soccer.

C. Table tennis.

D. Baseball.

* Mayan ('mɑjən) adj. 馬雅文化的　resemble (rɪ'zɛmbḷ) v. 相似
  fatal ('fetḷ) adj. 致命的　captain ('kæptɪn) n. 隊長
  decapitate (dɪ'kæpə,tet) v. 斬首；砍頭
  concubine ('kɑnkju,baɪn) n. 妾　victor ('vɪktə) n. 勝利者

51. (**B**) Turning to the sports scene, the President tops the headlines
tonight.　As you may all remember from last summer's news,
it was reported that the President was attacked by an
amphibious rabbit while on his fishing trip.　Well it appears
that the President has another enemy in the animal world,
and this time it is a horse.

(TONE)

Q: What happened to the President last summer?

A. He went rabbit hunting.

B. He was attacked by a rabbit.

C. He went fishing.

D. He went jogging.

* amphibious (æm'fɪbɪəs) *adj.* 水陸兩棲的

52. (**D**) Nowadays learning a foreign language is often one of the major topics of conversation in people's life, particularly at places where the need to learn the language is great.

(TONE)

Q: What are people talking about?

A. Learning English.

B. Learning conversation skills.

C. Learning about foreign places.

D. Learning a foreign language.

53. (**C**) A Western film is usually about keeping law and order among cowboys and other frontiersmen.　They were the first to move into the western parts of the U.S. when it was still inhabited by Indians.

(TONE)

Q: Who were the first inhabitants of the West?

A. Cowboys.

B. Frontiersmen.

C. Indians.

D. Film makers.

* frontiersman (frʌn'tɪrzmən) *n.* 拓荒者
inhabit (ɪn'hæbɪt) *v.* 居住
inhabitant (ɪn'hæbətənt) *n.* 居民

54. (**D**) In a few minutes, we will make a brief stop in Chungshang. If you are going on the Tamshui Line or the Mucha Line, please transfer here.

(TONE)
Q: Where is this announcement heard?
A. On a bus.
B. In a taxi.
C. On an airplane.
D. On the mass rapid transit system.

* transfer (træns'fɜ) v. 換車　　transit ('trænsɪt) n. 運送
mass rapid transit system 大衆捷運系統

55. (**D**) Please hold the line. Your call will be answered when a customer service clerk is available.

(TONE)
Q: Who is speaking?
A. A customer.
B. A boss.
C. A teacher.
D. An operator.

56. (**C**) Don't miss our sports program at Elmont Training Center. When you've finished a long day of work, enjoy tennis, use the sauna or go jogging. We have bikes and skates, too.

(TONE)
Q: Who would make this announcement?
A. A TV sports announcer.
B. A bike salesman.
C. A facility manager.
D. A teacher.

* sauna ('sɔnə) n. 三溫暖　　facility (fə'sɪlətɪ) n. 設施

57. (**B**) Enjoy the refreshing taste of Peltzers, brewed of the best hops, malt and barley. Peltzers is cooked slowly to bring out its rich flavor. Available on draft in Pittsburgh only.

(TONE)

Q: What product is this advertising?

A. Soup.

B. Beer.

C. Bread.

D. Soft drink.

* refreshing (rɪ'frɛʃɪŋ) *adj.* 令人神清氣爽的
brew (bru) *v.* 釀造
hop (hɑp) *n.* 蛇麻子 (使啤酒帶苦味的調味)
malt (mɔlt) *n.* 麥芽　barley ('bɑrlɪ) *n.* 大麥
flavor ('flevɚ) *n.* 味道　*on draft* 生啤酒

58. (**C**) I'm pleased to present Mary Lou Reynolds, the first woman to sell over one million dollars of insurance a month in company history. Mary Lou joined us out of high school and worked her way up the corporate ladder. Since 1991, Ms. Reynolds has headed the agent-training program.

(TONE)

Q: Where would this announcement be made?

A. At a history lecture.

B. At a company which buys insurance.

C. At a meeting of employees.

D. At a birthday party.

* insurance (ɪn'ʃjurəns) *n.* 保險
corporate ('kɔrprɪt) *adj.* 公司的

59. (**B**) I've just gotten off the phone, and the visit by President Peters
to Taipei is being moved up to the 14th. This means, he'll be
here on the 12th, just two days from now. We're still going
to open the Civic Avenue restaurant on his first day here.
To do this, half of the staff, instead of one third as previously
scheduled, at the Portfield restaurant will be temporarily
transferred to Civic Avenue.

(TONE)

Q: What change is being announced?

A. A trip to Taipei.

B. The number of employees.

C. The name of a restaurant.

D. The charges of rooms.

* civic ('sıvık) *adj.* 市民的　　avenue ('ævə,nju) *n.* 大道
as previously scheduled 正如事先安排
temporarily ('tɛmpə,rɛrəlɪ) *adv.* 暫時地
transfer (træns'fɝ) *v.* 轉調

60. (**A**) In local news, Sylvia Dotter passed away at the age of 87.
She was thought to be quite poor. When her landlord entered
her home, over $400,000 of stocks were discovered. A note
gave everything to St. Michael's Church.

(TONE)

Q: What was discovered?

A. The woman's wealth.

B. A note from a church.

C. Where the woman lived.

D. The woman's age.

* ***pass away*** 去世　　landlord ('læn(d),lɔrd) *n.* 房東
stock (stɑk) *n.* 股票

English Listening Comprehension Test

Test Book No. 5

   This listening comprehension test will test your ability to understand spoken English.   In this test, each conversation, statement and question will be spoken JUST ONE TIME.   They will not be written out for you.   There are four parts to this test.   Special instructions will be given to you at the beginning of each part.

Part A

   In Part A, you will see several pictures in your test book.   For each picture, you will be asked 1 to 3 questions.   For each question, you will hear four possible answers.   Choose the best answer according to what you see in the picture.

Example:

   You will see:

   You will hear: What is this?
                    A. This is a table.
                    B. This is a chair.
                    C. This is a watch.
                    D. This is a doll.

The best answer to the question "What is this?" is B: "This is a chair." Therefore, you should choose answer B.

A. <u>Questions 1-3</u>

D. <u>Questions 10-12</u>

B. <u>Questions 4-6</u>

E. <u>Question 13-15</u>

C. <u>Questions 7-9</u>

Part B

In Part B, you will hear 15 questions.   After you hear a question, read the four possible answers in your test book and decide which one is the best answer to the question you have heard.

Example:

<u>You will hear</u>:   What does your father do?

<u>You will read</u>:   A. He's 50 years old.
B. He's a teacher.
C. He's hungry.
D. He's in Los Angeles.

The best answer to the question "What does your father do?" is B: "He's a teacher."   Therefore, you should choose answer B.

Please go to the next page. ⇨

16. A. Very good.
    B. d-o-g — dog
    C. dog
    D. How are you?

17. A. For six hours.
    B. At six o'clock.
    C. Quite often.
    D. Yes, I do.

18. A. She walks to school.
    B. Yes, she walks to school.
    C. She doesn't walk to school.
    D. She goes to school every morning.

19. A. Very much.
    B. Those presents are very beautiful.
    C. They bought those presents at the store.
    D. No, they don't like those presents a lot.

20. A. I can't wait!
    B. I can't believe it!
    C. Oh, aren't they?
    D. Oh, I love it.

21. A. I have everything we'll need for camping.
    B. Where are the birds?
    C. I thought you brought the food.
    D. I'm sorry. I have an English test tomorrow.

22. A. You are welcome.
    B. Can I give you a hand?
    C. Camping at the lake can be exciting.
    D. I lost my car keys.

23. A. A little won't make you fat.
    B. Yes, I do.
    C. That's all right.
    D. No, thanks. I'm afraid of getting fat.

24. A. Please go to the next street.
    B. Every five minutes.
    C. You have to buy a ticket first.
    D. It is five dollars.

25. A. He often helps people.
    B. He is not lazy.
    C. I don't think so.
    D. I don't play with him.

26. A. I am glad to hear that.
    B. That's all right.
    C. He goes to the movies.
    D. He can play soccer.

27. A. I have no money.
    B. Oh, I don't know yet.
    C. I have two tickets.
    D. Can you go with me?

28. A. Yes, I can't.
    B. Neither do I.
    C. I want size 44.
    D. I can, too.

29. A. She accepts our idea now.
    B. I can't wait.
    C. You can tell her about this.
    D. She is kind to us.

30. A. Yes, I don't want to buy anything.
    B. I am sorry to trouble you.
    C. Yes, how much is this blue sweater?
    D. Of course, I'll give you a hand.

Part C

In Part C, you will hear 15 conversations between a man and a woman.   After each conversation, you will hear a question about the conversation.   After you hear the question, read the four possible answers in your test book and choose the best answer to the question you have heard.

Example:

You will hear: (Man)   How do you go to school every day?
(Woman)   Usually by bus.   Sometimes by taxi.

TONE: How does the woman go to school?

You will read: A. She always goes to school on foot.
B. She usually takes a bike.
C. She takes either a bus or a taxi.
D. She usually goes to school by bus, never by taxi.

The best answer to the question "How does the woman go to school?" is C: "She takes either a bus or a taxi."   Therefore, you should choose answer C.

Please go to the next page. ⇨

31. A. The snow storm in Michigan.
　　B. The winter weather in the midwest.
　　C. Departure of the flight.
　　D. Delay of the airplane.

32. A. He is an undergraduate student.
　　B. He studies mechanical engineering.
　　C. He is majoring in electrical engineering.
　　D. He is living in Mexico.

33. A. He would like to help the woman typing.
　　B. He wonders how much he should pay her.
　　C. He wants the woman to help him.
　　D. He prefers to type the paper by himself.

34. A. Tomorrow will be fine.
　　B. He is very upset.
　　C. It's going to be icy tomorrow.
　　D. The sky is going to be cloudy.

35. A. The woman needs the recipe which explains the amount of butter.
　　B. He is reminding the woman to buy butter.
　　C. This recipe requires two spoonfuls of butter.
　　D. He doesn't want the woman to use a lot of butter.

36. A. He saw a beauty queen in Paris.
　　B. Each city presents a queen for the beauty pageant.
　　C. There are many beautiful ladies in Paris.
　　D. Paris is the most attractive city of all.

37. A. Most of the students are majoring in statistics.
　　B. Statistics is an elective course for freshmen.
　　C. All economics majors must take statistics.
　　D. Students can elect either mathematics or statistics.

38. A. He is pleased to know she
    enjoys jogging.
    B. The car runs really well.
    C. It has been ten years since
    he bought the car.
    D. The car usually starts with
    a little trouble.

39. A. She was very frightened.
    B. She had a heart problem.
    C. She lost the race.
    D. Overall, she was happy.

40. A. Read geography I for
    tomorrow.
    B. Read the second chapter
    for tomorrow.
    C. Read Chapter One for
    tomorrow.
    D. Read two chapters for
    tomorrow.

41. A. Turn down the radio.
    B. Turn off the radio.
    C. Keep the radio on.
    D. Change the radio station.

42. A. Hand the book to John.
    B. Give a math lesson to John.
    C. Ask John some math
    questions.
    D. Help John with his math
    assignment.

43. A. Keep his weight as it is.
    B. Pay attention to what she
    eats.
    C. Eat food which has more
    calories.
    D. Not to eat desserts after
    meals.

44. A. We have to learn how to
    repair computers.
    B. Using a computer requires
    a lot of knowledge.
    C. We cannot let computers
    control us.
    D. We should live without
    depending upon the
    computer.

45. A. She can manage much
    more.
    B. She will take one.
    C. She doesn't care how
    many she gets.
    D. She will not take any.

Part D

In Part D, you will hear 15 short talks. After each talk, you will hear a question about the talk. After you hear the question, read the four possible answers in your test book and choose the best answer to the question you have heard.

Example:

You will hear: Well, that's all for Unit 15. For today's
                  homework, please do the review questions on
                  page 80, and we'll check the answers tomorrow.
                  Now, let's go on to Unit 16.

                  TONE: What is the teacher going to do next in
                        today's class?

You will read: A. Check the homework.
                  B. Review Unit 15.
                  C. Start a new unit.
                  D. Answer students' questions.

The best answer to the question "What is the teacher going to do next in today's class?" is C: "Start a new unit." Therefore, you should choose answer C.

Please go to the next page. ⇨

46. A. Spain.
    B. France.
    C. The Royal Hospital.
    D. Paris.

47. A. A referee.
    B. A sports announcer.
    C. A coach.
    D. A student.

48. A. Music.
    B. Literature.
    C. Dance.
    D. Painting.

49. A. Salad.
    B. Soup.
    C. Dinner.
    D. Dessert.

50. A. A lower unemployment rate.
    B. A new television program.
    C. A redevelopment project.
    D. A construction contract.

51. A. An essay.
    B. A magazine article.
    C. A poem.
    D. A short story.

52. A. The stage.
    B. London.
    C. England.
    D. The cinema.

53. A. In the park.
    B. By a famous landmark.
    C. In the museum dining room.
    D. Near the docks.

54. A. Pick up the phone right away.
    B. Take your seat immediately.
    C. Apply as soon as you can.
    D. Pay next month.

55. A. Many coats were lost.
    B. Some people forgot their tags.
    C. Many coats were destroyed.
    D. A confusing system was used.

56. A. To conserve energy.
    B. To save water.
    C. To report consumer fraud.
    D. To lock their doors.

57. A. A recording.
    B. A directory.
    C. A caller.
    D. A student.

58. A. Rent equipment.
    B. Sweep the ice.
    C. Buy jackets.
    D. Leave the arena.

59. A. Individuals can help very little.
    B. Recycling newspapers and glass is the answer.
    C. Economists must participate.
    D. Everyone should help.

60. A. There are many small farms.
    B. Only university graduates can become farmers.
    C. Farming is not a popular subject in school.
    D. Farming is a big business.

Listening Test 5 詳解

Part A

For questions number 1 to 3, please look at picture A.

1. (**B**) Question number 1, where are the men?
    A. They are in a bus.
    B. They are in a hotel.
    C. They are in a hospital.
    D. They are in a library.

2. (**C**) Question number 2, please look at picture A again. Who is the man behind the counter?
    A. He is a customer.
    B. He is a waiter.
    C. He is a receptionist.
    D. He is a librarian.

    * receptionist (rɪ'sɛpʃənɪst) *n.* 接待員

3. (**C**) Question number 3, please look at picture A again. What is the man in front of the counter doing?
    A. He is sitting.
    B. He is reading and writing.
    C. He is writing and smoking.
    D. He is ordering food.

For questions number 4 to 6, please look at picture B.

4. (**C**) Question number 4, what are they drinking?
    A. They are drinking tea.
    B. They are drinking juice.
    C. They are drinking coffee.
    D. They are drinking water.

5. (**A**) Question number 5, please look at picture B again.　What is the man reading?

    A. He is reading a newspaper.

    B. He is reading a magazine.

    C. He is reading a book.

    D. He is reading a bill.

    * bill〔bɪl〕*n.* 帳單

6. (**B**) Question number 6, please look at picture B again.　What did the man do with the coffee?

    A. He drank it.

    B. He spilt it.

    C. He made it.

    D. He threw it.

    * spill〔spɪl〕*v.* 潑灑（過去式為 spilt 或 spilled）

For questions number 7 to 9, please look at picture C.

7. (**C**) Question number 7, where are they?

    A. They are at home.

    B. They are at school.

    C. They are in an office.

    D. They are at a restaurant.

8. (**C**) Question number 8, please look at picture C again.　What are they looking at?

    A. They are looking at some papers.

    B. They are looking at a clock.

    C. They are looking at a calendar.

    D. They are looking at a notebook.

9. (**B**) Question number 9, please look at picture C again.
Which month is it?
  A. It is the first month.
  B. It is the fifth month.
  C. It is the eighth month.
  D. It is the fourth month.

For questions number 10 to 12, please look at picture D.

10. (**D**) Question number 10, what did the waiter do?
  A. He made some water.
  B. He threw some water.
  C. He poured some water.
  D. He spilled some water.

11. (**A**) Question number 11, please look at picture D again.
How does the customer feel?
  A. He is surprised.
  B. He is delighted.
  C. He is satisfied.
  D. He is relaxed.

12. (**C**) Question number 12, please look at picture D again.
What did the man order?
  A. Coffee.
  B. Steak.
  C. We do not know.
  D. Pizza.

For questions number 13 to 15, please look at picture E.

13. (**B**) Question number 13, what does the customer have?
  A. The customer has a bear.
  B. The customer has a mustache.
  C. The customer has a towel.
  D. The customer has a razor.

  * mustache (ˈmʌstæʃ) n. 髭   razor (ˈrezə) n. 剃刀

14. (**A**) Question number 14, please look at picture E again.　Who is the man behind the customer?

A. He is a barber.

B. He is a plumber.

C. He is a doctor.

D. He is a carpenter.

* barber ('bɑrbɚ) *n.* 理髮師　　plumber ('plʌmɚ) *n.* 水管工人
carpenter ('kɑrpəntɚ) *n.* 木匠

15. (**D**) Question number 15, please look at picture E again.　What is the customer doing?

A. He is having his hair cut.

B. He is having his hair washed.

C. He is having a massage.

D. He is having a shave.

* massage (mə'sɑʒ) *n.* 按摩

Part B

16. (**C**) Say the word "dog", Bill.

A. Very good.

B. d-o-g — dog

C. dog

D. How are you?

17. (**B**) What time do you get up every morning?

A. For six hours.

B. At six o'clock.

C. Quite often.

D. Yes, I do.

18. (**A**) How does Helen go to school?

A. She walks to school.

B. Yes, she walks to school.

C. She doesn't walk to school.

D. She goes to school every morning.

19. (**A**) How do they like those presents?
      A. Very much.
      B. Those presents are very beautiful.
      C. They bought those presents at the store.
      D. No, they don't like those presents a lot.

20. (**B**) All those over there are my sister's hats.
      A. I can't wait!
      B. I can't believe it!
      C. Oh, aren't they?
      D. Oh, I love it.

21. (**D**) Let's go fishing, all right?
      A. I have everything we'll need for camping.
      B. Where are the birds?
      C. I thought you brought the food.
      D. I'm sorry. I have an English test tomorrow.

22. (**D**) May, you don't look very happy.　Is anything wrong?
      A. You are welcome.
      B. Can I give you a hand?
      C. Camping at the lake can be exciting.
      D. I lost my car keys.
      * *gave sb. a hand* 幫助某人

23. (**D**) Would you like some ice cream?
      A. A little won't make you fat.
      B. Yes, I do.
      C. That's all right.
      D. No, thanks. I'm afraid of getting fat.

24. (**A**) Where can I take a bus to the zoo?
      A. Please go to the next street.
      B. Every five minutes.
      C. You have to buy a ticket first.
      D. It is five dollars.

25. (**C**)　Ted is a bad boy, isn't he?
　　　A. He often helps people.
　　　B. He is not lazy.
　　　C. I don't think so.
　　　D. I don't play with him.

26. (**B**)　I am really sorry.
　　　A. I am glad to hear that.
　　　B. That's all right.
　　　C. He goes to the movies.
　　　D. He can play soccer.
　　　* soccer ('sɑkɚ) *n.* 足球

27. (**B**)　What are you going to do tomorrow?
　　　A. I have no money.
　　　B. Oh, I don't know yet.
　　　C. I have two tickets.
　　　D. Can you go with me?

28. (**B**)　I don't know where you can find a size as big as that.
　　　A. Yes, I can't.
　　　B. Neither do I.
　　　C. I want size 44.
　　　D. I can, too.

29. (**A**)　Does the teacher agree with you?
　　　A. She accepts our idea now.
　　　B. I can't wait.
　　　C. You can tell her about this.
　　　D. She is kind to us.

30. (**C**)　Can I help you?
　　　A. Yes, I don't want to buy anything.
　　　B. I am sorry to trouble you.
　　　C. Yes, how much is this blue sweater?
　　　D. Of course, I'll give you a hand.

Part C

31. (**D**) W: What did the announcement say?
　　　　 M: The weather is bad; consequently, the flight was delayed.

　　　 (TONE)
　　　 Q: What was the announcement about?
　　　 A. The snow storm in Michigan.
　　　 B. The winter weather in the midwest.
　　　 C. Departure of the flight.
　　　 D. Delay of the airplane.

　　　 * delay (dɪ'le) v. 延誤　　 departure (dɪ'pɑrtʃɚ) n. 離開

32. (**C**) W: I saw a new student at the cafeteria this afternoon.　Have
　　　　　 you met him?
　　　　 M: Yes, Arthur Maso, a student from Mexico, is a graduate
　　　　　 student in electrical engineering.

　　　 (TONE)
　　　 Q: What does the man say about Arthur?
　　　 A. He is an undergraduate student.
　　　 B. He studies mechanical engineering.
　　　 C. He is majoring in electrical engineering.
　　　 D. He is living in Mexico.

　　　 * cafeteria (,kæfə'tɪrɪə) n. 自助餐廳　　 *graduate student* 研究生
　　　 electrical engineering 電子工程　　 *undergraduate student* 大學部學生

33. (**C**) W: Would you like me to type your paper this time?
　　　　 M: Would I?　Please do.

　　　 (TONE)
　　　 What does the man mean?
　　　 A. He would like to help the woman typing.
　　　 B. He wonders how much he should pay her.
　　　 C. He wants the woman to help him.
　　　 D. He prefers to type the paper by himself.

Listening Test 5 詳解 5-19

34. (**A**) W: Did you listen to the weather report on the radio?
    M: Yes, the weather forecast is for blue skies tomorrow.

    (TONE)
    Q: What does the man mean?
    A. Tomorrow will be fine.
    B. He is very upset.
    C. It's going to be icy tomorrow.
    D. The sky is going to be cloudy.

    * forecast (ˈforˌkæst) *n.* 預測   upset (ʌpˈsɛt) *adj.* 心煩的
    icy (ˈaɪsɪ) *adj.* 冰冷的

35. (**C**) M: Don't forget that this recipe calls for two spoonfuls of butter.
    W: Oh, no, what shall I do? I ran out of it.

    (TONE)
    Q: What does the man mean?
    A. The woman needs the recipe which explains the amount
       of butter.
    B. He is reminding the woman to buy butter.
    C. This recipe requires two spoonfuls of butter.
    D. He doesn't want the woman to use a lot of butter.

    * recipe (ˈrɛsəpɪ) *n.* 食譜   spoonful (ˈspunˌful) *n.* 一匙（之量）
    run out of 用完

36. (**D**) W: I heard you were in Paris during the summer. Did you
       enjoy Paris?
    M: Oh, yes! She's a queen among cities.

    (TONE)
    Q: What does the man mean?
    A. He saw a beauty queen in Paris.
    B. Each city presents a queen for the beauty pageant.
    C. There are many beautiful ladies in Paris.
    D. Paris is the most attractive city of all.

    * pageant (ˈpædʒənt) *n.* 花車遊行

37. (**C**) W: I know freshman mathematics and physics but do you know about statistics?

M: Statistics is a required course for majors in economics.

(TONE)

Q: What is the man saying about statistics?

A. Most of the students are majoring in statistics.

B. Statistics is an elective course for freshmen.

C. All economics majors must take statistics.

D. Students can elect either mathematics or statistics.

* statistics (stə'tɪstɪks) n. 統計學　　*required course* 必修課
major ('medʒɚ) n. 主修生

38. (**B**) W: How is the car that you bought from me last year? I had used it for ten years, you know.

M: Oh, she is running like a dream these days.

(TONE)

Q: What does the man mean?

A. He is pleased to know she enjoys jogging.

B. The car runs really well.

C. It has been ten years since he bought the car.

D. The car usually starts with a little trouble.

* dream (drim) n. 美好的事物

39. (**A**) M: You weren't scared, were you?

W: Not much, I wasn't! My heart was beating fast and tears were running down my face, that's all.

(TONE)

Q: What does the woman mean?

A. She was very frightened.

B. She had a heart problem.

C. She lost the race.

D. Overall, she was happy.

* scared (skɛrd) adj. 受到驚嚇的

40. (**B**) M: I forgot the geography assignment. Could you tell me what it was?

W: Certainly. Professor Smith asked us to read the second chapter for tomorrow.

(TONE)

Q: What is their homework?

A. Read geography I for tomorrow.

B. Read the second chapter for tomorrow.

C. Read Chapter One for tomorrow.

D. Read two chapters for tomorrow.

* geography (dʒɪˈɑgrəfɪ) *n.* 地理學
assignment (əˈsaɪnmənt) *n.* 指定作業

41. (**C**) W: Shall I turn off the radio?

M: No, please don't.

(TONE)

Q: What will the woman do?

A. Turn down the radio.

B. Turn off the radio.

C. Keep the radio on.

D. Change the radio station.

* *turn off* 關掉　　*turn down* 音量轉小　　*radio station* 廣播頻道

42. (**A**) W: If John asks you for this math textbook, will you give it to him?

M: I sure will. When is he coming?

(TONE)

Q: What does the woman want the man to do?

A. Hand the book to John.

B. Give a math lesson to John.

C. Ask John some math questions.

D. Help John with his math assignment.

* textbook (ˈtɛkstˌbuk) *n.* 課本

43. (**D**) M: What do you have for dessert?

　　　　W: Can't you do without desserts in order to lose weight?

　　　　(TONE)

　　　　Q: What does the woman want the man to do?

　　　　A. Keep his weight as it is.

　　　　B. Pay attention to what she eats.

　　　　C. Eat food which has more calories.

　　　　D. Not to eat desserts after meals.

　　　　* dessert (dɪ'zɝt) *n.* 甜點心　　*lose weight* 減輕體重
　　　　calory ('kælərɪ) *n.* 卡路里

44. (**C**) W: We can't live without the computer these days, can we?

　　　　M: Yes, but the important thing to remember is that we've got
　　　　　　to become its master.

　　　　(TONE)

　　　　Q: What does man mean?

　　　　A. We have to learn how to repair computers.

　　　　B. Using a computer requires a lot of knowledge.

　　　　C. We cannot let computers control us.

　　　　D. We should live without depending upon the computer.

45. (**B**) M: You really shouldn't take any more.

　　　　W: Well, one more, and then no more.

　　　　(TONE)

　　　　Q: What does the woman mean?

　　　　A. She can manage much more.

　　　　B. She will take one.

　　　　C. She doesn't care how many she gets.

　　　　D. She will not take any.

Part D

46. (**A**) Picasso, the famous Spanish painter, was born in 1881.
His father was an art teacher. Picasso began to paint very
early. He was admitted to the Royal Academy of Art at the age
of 15. After 1900, he spent much time in Paris, living there
from 1904 to 1947, when he moved to the south of France.

(TONE)
Q: Where was Piccaso born?
A. Spain.
B. France.
C. The Royal Hospital.
D. Paris.

47. (**C**) So far, we've been able to keep to our game plan. We've
avoided penalties that would leave us shorthanded. Their
goalie has blocked all of our shots, but he can't keep doing
that much longer. Go out there now and put some points on
the scoreboard.

(TONE)
Q: Who is speaking?
A. A referee.
B. A sports announcer.
C. A coach.
D. A student.

* penalty ('pɛnltɪ) *n.* 處罰　　shorthanded ('ʃɔrt'hændɪd) *adj.* 人手不足的
goalie ('golɪ) *n.* 守門員　　scoreboard ('skor,bord) *n.* 計分板
referee (,rɛfə'ri) *n.* 裁判　　announcer (ə'naʊnsɚ) *n.* 廣播員
coach (kotʃ) *n.* 教練

48. (**A**) Today we are going to listen to one of the greatest musical
pieces ever composed. But before we begin listening to this
piece of work by Beethoven, I would like to introduce the life
of this great musician.

(TONE)

Q: What is this lecture about?

A. Music.

B. Literature.

C. Dance.

D. Painting.

49. (**B**) Westerners eat their food in the following order: first, the appetizer, second, the soup, third, the dinner itself, fourth, salad, and finally, dessert and tea or coffee.

(TONE)

Q: What is the second thing westerners eat?

A. Salad.

B. Soup.

C. Dinner.

D. Dessert.

* appetizer (ˈæpəˌtaɪzɚ) *n.* 開胃菜

50. (**C**) The old Vincent television plant will be turned into a fish canning plant which will employ 200 workers. The old Vincent plant employed ten times that number, so the unemployment rate is still expected to remain unchanged.

(TONE)

Q: What is being announced?

A. A lower unemployment rate.

B. A new television program.

C. A redevelopment project.

D. A construction contract.

* plant (plænt) *n.* 工廠　　***unemployment rate*** 失業率

51. (**D**) If you have any questions at any time, you can see me on Tuesdays.　My office is on the second floor of this building. Your assignment for Wednesday is to read Hemingway's short story on page 55.

(TONE)
Q: What must the students read for Wednesday?

A. An essay.
B. A magazine article.
C. A poem.
D. A short story.

＊ article ('ɑrtɪkl) n. 文章

52. (**B**) Theater is a highly developed art form especially in England where London is the center.　Theater nowadays is very expensive and very popular, so for many people, going to the theater is a special occasion.

(TONE)
Q: Which place is a center for theater?

A. The stage.
B. London.
C. England.
D. The cinema.

＊ cinema ('sɪnəmə) n. 電影

53. (**D**) After driving through what I'm sure you'll agree is the most beautiful park you've ever been in, we'll stop off for a superb seafood dinner on the wharf.　You might be tired by tonight, but I guarantee that you'll feel like you had a real vacation.

(TONE)

Q: Where will the group end its tour?

A. In the park.

B. By a famous landmark.

C. In the museum dining room.

D. Near the docks.

* superb (su'pɝb) adj. 一流的　　wharf (hwɔrf) n. 碼頭
　　tour (tur) n. 遊覽　　dock (dɑk) n. 碼頭

54. (**C**) Enrollment in these programs is limited and early application
is essential, since our programs often have a waiting list.　If
any of you new students need these services, please let me
know right away so I can get you an application form.

(TONE)

Q: What does the speaker recommend?

A. Pick up the phone right away.

B. Take your seat immediately.

C. Apply as soon as you can.

D. Pay next month.

* enrollment (in'rolmənt) n. 登記　　essential (ɪ'sɛnʃəl) adj. 必要的
　　waiting list 後補名單

55. (**D**) The coat check room has given each of you a numbered plastic
tag.　Unfortunately, two different sets of tags were used.
Be sure your tag is the same color as the coat check's tag
with that number.　If you're picking up a coat for someone,
be careful that you don't make a mistake.

(TONE)

Q: What has happened?

A. Many coats were lost.

B. Some people forgot their tags.

C. Many coats were destroyed.

D. A confusing system was used.

* **check room** （物品）寄存處　　**plastic tag** 塑膠牌

56. (**B**) Severe drought conditions cause mandatory water conservation measures to remain in effect.　Officials of the water conservation district are patrolling neighborhoods ticketing violators.　Consumers failing to limit their use face penalties or even disruption of service.

(TONE)

Q: What are people asked to do?

A. To conserve energy.

B. To save water.

C. To report consumer fraud.

D. To lock their doors.

* severe (sə'vɪr) *adj.* 嚴重的　　drought (draʊt) *n.* 乾旱
mandatory ('mændə,torɪ) *adj.* 強制的　***water conservation*** 節約用水
in effect 有效的　　district ('dɪstrɪkt) *n.* 區
patrol (pə'trol) *v.* 巡查　　ticket ('tɪkɪt) *v.* 開罰單
violator ('vaɪə,letə) *n.* 違規者　***fail to*** 未能
disruption (dɪs'rʌpʃən) *n.* 中斷　　fraud (frɔd) *n.* 欺騙 (行為)

57. (**A**) We're sorry, the number you have dialed, 2345-5543 is no longer in service.　Please check your telephone directory or hold the line for an operator.

(TONE)

Q: Who is speaking?

A. A recording.

B. A directory.

C. A caller.

D. A student.

* directory (də'rɛktərɪ) *n.* 電話簿

58. (**D**) Cragon Arena will be closing in 15 minutes.　Please clear the ice.　Return all rented skates to the pro shop.　Pick up all belongings.　Don't forget skates, jackets and bags when you go.

(TONE)

Q: What should people do now?

A. Rent equipment.

B. Sweep the ice.

C. Buy jackets.

D. Leave the arena.

  * skate〔sket〕*n.* 冰鞋　　***pro shop*** 雜貨販售店（= *provision shop*）
    arena〔ə'rɪnə〕*n.* 場地

59. (**D**) In order to help conserve our dwindling natural resources,
we will need every-one's help and cooperation, in such ventures
as recycling newspapers and glass so that they can be used again.

(TONE)

Q: What does the speaker suggest regarding conservation?

A. Individuals can help very little.

B. Recycling newspapers and glass is the answer.

C. Economists must participate.

D. Everyone should help.

  * dwindling（'dwɪndlɪŋ）*adj.* 漸減少的　　venture（'vɛntʃə）*n.* 事業
    recycle〔ri'saɪkḷ〕*v.* 再生利用

60. (**D**) Nowadays, farming has become a big business, and the farmers
must buy a lot of big and expensive machines.　An ever
growing number of college and university students are involved
in farming.

(TONE)

Q: According to the speaker, which statement is true?

A. There are many small farms.

B. Only university graduates can become farmers.

C. Farming is not a popular subject in school.

D. Farming is a big business.

  * ***be involved in*** 熱中於

English Listening Comprehension Test

Test Book No. 6

This listening comprehension test will test your ability to understand spoken English. In this test, each conversation, statement and question will be spoken JUST ONE TIME. They will not be written out for you. There are four parts to this test. Special instructions will be given to you at the beginning of each part.

Part A

In Part A, you will see several pictures in your test book. For each picture, you will be asked 1 to 3 questions. For each question, you will hear four possible answers. Choose the best answer according to what you see in the picture.

Example:

You will see:

You will hear: What is this?
A. This is a table.
B. This is a chair.
C. This is a watch.
D. This is a doll.

The best answer to the question "What is this?" is B: "This is a chair." Therefore, you should choose answer B.

A. Questions 1-3

D. Questions 10-12

B. Questions 4-6

E. Questions 13-14

C. Questions 7-9

F. Question 15

Part B

In Part B, you will hear 15 questions. After you hear a question, read the four possible answers in your test book and decide which one is the best answer to the question you have heard.

Example:

<u>You will hear:</u>   What does your father do?

<u>You will read:</u>   A. He's 50 years old.
B. He's a teacher.
C. He's hungry.
D. He's in Los Angeles.

The best answer to the question "What does your father do?" is B: "He's a teacher." Therefore, you should choose answer B.

Please go to the next page. ⇨

16. A. Why do you come to me?
    B. I know you will come.
    C. That's your problem.
    D. What's the matter?

17. A. So am I.
    B. It is your night.
    C. It's not mine, either.
    D. I don't like your day.

18. A. I think it looks like
       medicine.
    B. It tastes delicious.
    C. I taste it carefully.
    D. Yes, it's very good.

19. A. Yes, I am.
    B. No, I'm not playing.
    C. Yes, we're watching TV.
    D. No, we're playing.

20. A. Yes, I never.
    B. Of course, I don't.
    C. Sure, I do.
    D. Why? I don't, either.

21. A. I don't, either.
    B. Mind your own business.
    C. That's not a good habit.
    D. Can you give me a hand?

22. A. It's late.
    B. It leaves at 3:00.
    C. I'll see you then.
    D. It takes a lot of time.

23. A. I'd love to.
    B. I can't believe it.
    C. Why not me?
    D. Certainly, I wouldn't.

24. A. Fine, how do you do?
    B. Fine, nice to know you,
       John.
    C. Oh, fine, it is kind of you.
    D. I am fine. Thank you.
       How are you?

25. A. Yes, it's English.
    B. No, the second class.
    C. No, you're right.
    D. Yes, I speak good Chinese.

26. A. Not the television.
    B. The sofas are.
    C. They are chairs.
    D. It's not a desk.

27. A. It is hot in summer.
    B. It is summer.
    C. It's Sunday.
    D. I like summer very much.

28. A. Yes, there is.
    B. Yes, there is not.
    C. Please turn off the light.
    D. I do not mean it.

29. A. Everything was on sale.
    B. We didn't even sell a bun.
    C. We didn't have to pay
       anything.
    D. Our boss thought much
       about our customers.

30. A. We can't wait!
    B. That's too bad.
    C. Really? Why did they
       buy another TV?
    D. I wish it's ours.

Part C

In Part C, you will hear 15 conversations between a man and a woman. After each conversation, you will hear a question about the conversation. After you hear the question, read the four possible answers in your test book and choose the best answer to the question you have heard.

Example:

You will hear: (Man)   How do you go to school every day?
(Woman) Usually by bus. Sometimes by taxi.

TONE: How does the woman go to school?

You will read: A. She always goes to school on foot.
B. She usually takes a bike.
C. She takes either a bus or a taxi.
D. She usually goes to school by bus, never by taxi.

The best answer to the question "How does the woman go to school?" is C: "She takes either a bus or a taxi." Therefore, you should choose answer C.

Please go to the next page. ⇨

31. A. She should try on one or
    two sweaters.
  B. She must buy one or two
    sweaters.
  C. She should be ready to
    take two sweaters home.
  D. She should select one of
    the best sweaters.

32. A. She doesn't know how
    she is doing in French.
  B. Her four skills of
    French are highly
    improved.
  C. Her speaking ability is
    average.
  D. She can't manage the
    course as much as she
    wants to.

33. A. He doesn't know if Mr.
    Lee was born in
    Indonesia.
  B. He doesn't know where
    Mr. Lee lived before.
  C. He doesn't know when
    Mr. Lee will go to Hong
    Kong.
  D. He doesn't know where
    Mr. Lee grew up.

34. A. He wants the woman to
    borrow his book.
  B. He suggests that she find the
    book if she wants to borrow it.
  C. If she had found the book,
    she could have.
  D. He brought the book home,
    but it's disappeared.

35. A. He is folding his napkin.
  B. He is looking for his fork.
  C. He is eating food without
    a fork.
  D. He is becoming frustrated
    because he can't find his
    napkin.

36. A. He thinks she is an excellent
    teacher.
  B. The new teacher is obnoxious.
  C. There should be a better
    teacher than she.
  D. She is a very rude teacher.

37. A. To the movies.
  B. To the flower garden.
  C. To the concert.
  D. To the zoo.

38. A. Order a sofa this afternoon.
  B. Send a catalog of sofas.
  C. Deliver a sofa.
  D. Sit on a sofa.

39. A. He can't swing a golf club well.
    B. He hurt his back.
    C. He used to be a good golfer, but is not any more.
    D. He always has a backache.

40. A. Jason Daniels isn't home right now.
    B. The man dialed the wrong number.
    C. Jason Daniels can't come to the phone right now.
    D. Jason Daniels doesn't want to speak to the caller.

41. A. He is a coffee drinker.
    B. He likes to drink tea.
    C. He wants a coffee refill.
    D. Coffee makes him sick.

42. A. She feels that the man must go there by himself.
    B. She is complaining about standing in line and waiting.
    C. She is disappointed that the cafeteria is always crowded.
    D. She feels she should stand in line.

43. A. Everyone will enjoy the game today.
    B. It's nice weather.
    C. Tomorrow will be better weather.
    D. He expected better weather.

44. A. She feels that he should go on a diet.
    B. She thinks that he must become a vegetarian.
    C. She is surprised that he is not heavy.
    D. She is upset that he is overweight.

45. A. The beautiful scene that he has never seen before is breathtaking.
    B. The river appears to flow in the opposite direction.
    C. The river starts from a lake.
    D. The mountain range gives rise to many streams.

Part D

In Part D, you will hear 15 short talks. After each talk, you will hear a question about the talk. After you hear the question, read the four possible answers in your test book and choose the best answer to the question you have heard.

Example:

<u>You will hear</u>: Well, that's all for Unit 15. For today's homework, please do the review questions on page 80, and we'll check the answers tomorrow. Now, let's go on to Unit 16.

TONE: What is the teacher going to do next in today's class?

<u>You will read</u>: A. Check the homework.
B. Review Unit 15.
C. Start a new unit.
D. Answer students' questions.

The best answer to the question "What is the teacher going to do next in today's class?" is C: "Start a new unit." Therefore, you should choose answer C.

Please go to the next page. ⇨

46. A. Donald Duck.
    B. Pluto.
    C. Snow White.
    D. Goofy.

47. A. For 15 minutes.
    B. For one hour.
    C. All night long.
    D. For two hours.

48. A. The tickets are all sold out.
    B. The ceiling of the theater is leaking.
    C. The movie is not very funny.
    D. The film has been misplaced.

49. A. A menu.
    B. A set-price dinner.
    C. A table.
    D. A dessert.

50. A. One day.
    B. Three days.
    C. Six days.
    D. Eleven days.

51. A. They make exciting writing.
    B. They help to sell papers.
    C. People hate to read these articles.
    D. UFOs are rare stories.

52. A. A pupil.
    B. A biology professor.
    C. An eye specialist.
    D. A safety expert.

53. A. 20.
    B. More than 20.
    C. Less than 20.
    D. 7.

54. A. To help Ms. Williamson
    find the Lost and Found
    Center.
    B. To tell Ms. Williamson
    that she has a telephone
    call.
    C. To bring Ms. Williamson
    to the Lost and Found
    Center.
    D. To report that Ms.
    Williamson is lost.

55. A. A flight schedule.
    B. Dinner in a restaurant.
    C. A train.
    D. A bus.

56. A. At a board of directors
    meeting.
    B. At a courier service
    counter.
    C. At a contract signing
    ceremony.
    D. At a funeral ceremony.

57. A. A newspaper.
    B. A radio station.
    C. A telephone company.
    D. A magazine.

58. A. He is trying to make a
    serious proposal.
    B. He is trying to ask for
    information.
    C. He is trying to amuse the
    audience.
    D. He is trying to warn the
    audience.

59. A. Consumers.
    B. Doctors.
    C. Farmers.
    D. Students.

60. A. To inform people of the
    zoo show.
    B. To announce the zoo will
    close soon.
    C. To advertise goods sold
    at the gift shop.
    D. To promote a restaurant
    serving lunch at the zoo.

Listening Test 6 詳解

Part A

For questions number 1 to 3, please look at picture A.

1. (**D**) Question number 1, where are the women?
  A. They are in a restaurant.
  B. They are in a rest room.
  C. They are in a department store.
  D. They are in a beauty parlor.
  * **rest room** 廁所 parlor ('parlɚ) *n.* 店 ***beauty parlor*** 美容院

2. (**C**) Question number 2, please look at picture A again. What is the customer doing?
  A. She is combing her hair.
  B. She is taking a shower.
  C. She is reading.
  D. She is eating.
  * comb (kom) *v.* 梳

3. (**D**) Question number 3, please look at picture A again. What is the customer's hairstyle?
  A. The customer has long hair.
  B. The customer has dark hair.
  C. The customer has straight hair.
  D. The customer has wavy hair.
  * wavy ('wevɪ) *adj.* 波浪形的

For questions number 4 to 6, please look at picture B.

4. (**D**) Question number 4, where are these two women?
  A. They are in a store.
  B. They are in a health club.
  C. They are in an airport.
  D. They are in a post office.
  * ***health club*** 健身中心

5. (**B**) Question number 5, please look at picture B again. Where is the package?

    A. The package is on a thermometer.

    B. The package is on a scale.

    C. The package is on a radar.

    D. The package is on a calculator.

    * thermometer (θə'mɑmətɚ) *n.* 溫度計   scale (skel) *n.* 磅秤
    radar ('redɑr) *n.* 雷達   calculator ('kælkjə‚letɚ) *n.* 計算機

6. (**D**) Question number 6, please look at picture B again. What is the clerk doing?

    A. The clerk is measuring a package.

    B. The clerk is selling a package.

    C. The clerk is buying a package.

    D. The clerk is weighing a package.

    * clerk (klɜk) *n.* 職員   weigh (we) *v.* 稱重

For questions number 7 to 9, please look at picture C.

7. (**B**) Question number 7, what is the man at the counter buying?

    A. He is buying a package.

    B. He is buying some stamps.

    C. He is buying an envelope.

    D. He is buying a scale.

    * counter ('kauntɚ) *n.* 櫃台

8. (**B**) Question number 8, please look at picture C again. Where is the little girl standing?

    A. She is standing at the front of the line.

    B. She is standing at the end of the line.

    C. She is standing in the middle of the line.

    D. She is standing at the door.

9. (**C**) Question number 9, please look at picture C again. What is the postman opening?

    A. He is opening a letter.

    B. He is opening a safe.

    C. He is opening a post box.

    D. He is opening a bag.

    * safe (sef) *n.* 保險箱

For questions number 10 to 12, please look at picture D.

10. (**B**) Question number 10, what is the man wearing?

    A. The man is wearing a sweater.

    B. The man is wearing a suit.

    C. The man is wearing shorts.

    D. The man is wearing an overcoat.

    * suit (sut) *n.* 西裝   shorts (ʃɔrts) *n.pl.* 短褲
    overcoat (,ovə'kot) *n.* 大衣

11. (**A**) Question number 11, please look at picture D again. What does the man want to buy?

    A. He wants to buy a shirt.

    B. He wants to buy shorts.

    C. He wants to buy a suit.

    D. He wants to buy a present for his wife.

12. (**B**) Question number 12, please look at picture D again. What else could the man buy here?

    A. He could also buy a skirt here.

    B. He could also buy a tie here.

    C. He could also buy a stereo here.

    D. He could also buy a sofa here.

    * stereo ('stɛrɪo) *n.* 音響

For questions number 13 to 14, please look at picture E.

13. (**B**) Question number 13, what is this a picture of?

    A. This is a picture of a department store.

    B. This is a picture of a hotel lobby.

    C. This is a picture of a restaurant.

    D. This is a picture of a post office.

14. (**C**) Question number 14, please look at picture E again.　What is the woman at the front desk doing?

    A. She is greeting the guests and opening the door.

    B. She is carrying the guests' luggage to their rooms.

    C. She is collecting payments from the guests.

    D. She is talking on the telephone.

    * *front desk* 櫃台　　greet (grit) *v.* 迎接　　payment ('pemənt) *n.* 付款

For question number 15, please look at picture F.

15. (**B**) Question number 15, what is the mother stirring?

    A. The mother is stirring the campfire.

    B. The mother is stirring the soup.

    C. The mother is stirring the sleeping bag.

    D. The mother is stirring the tent.

    * stir (stɝ) *v.* 攪動　　campfire ('kæmp,faɪr) *n.* 營火
    sleeping bag 睡袋　　tent (tɛnt) *n.* 帳蓬

Part B

16. (**D**) I'm not feeling very well, Doctor.

    A. Why do you come to me?

    B. I know you will come.

    C. That's your problem.

    D. What's the matter?

17. (**C**) This really isn't my day.

    A. So am I.
    B. It is your night.
    C. It's not mine, either.
    D. I don't like your day.

    * ***Today is not my day***. 我今天真倒楣。

18. (**B**) How does the food taste?

    A. I think it looks like medicine.
    B. It tastes delicious.
    C. I taste it carefully.
    D. Yes, it's very good.

19. (**D**) Are you studying, boys?

    A. Yes, I am.
    B. No, I'm not playing.
    C. Yes, we're watching TV.
    D. No, we're playing.

20. (**C**) Don't you ever use a tape recorder in school?

    A. Yes, I never.
    B. Of course, I don't.
    C. Sure, I do.
    D. Why? I don't, either.

21. (**C**) I like to study on the bed.

    A. I don't, either.
    B. Mind your own business.
    C. That's not a good habit.
    D. Can you give me a hand?

    * ***Mind your own business***. 少管閒事。   ***give sb. a hand*** 幫助某人

22. (**B**) What time is your flight?
  A. It's late.
  B. It leaves at 3:00.
  C. I'll see you then.
  D. It takes a lot of time.
  * flight〔flaɪt〕*n.* 班機

23. (**A**) Paul, would you like to sing us a Chinese song?
  A. I'd love to.
  B. I can't believe it.
  C. Why not me?
  D. Certainly, I wouldn't.

24. (**D**) Hi, how are you, Tom?
  A. Fine, how do you do?
  B. Fine, nice to know you, John.
  C. Oh, fine, it is kind of you.
  D. I am fine. Thank you. How are you?

25. (**B**) Is your first class Chinese?
  A. Yes, it's English.
  B. No, the second class.
  C. No, you're right.
  D. Yes, I speak good Chinese.

26. (**B**) What is near the door?
  A. Not the television.
  B. The sofas are.
  C. They are chairs.
  D. It's not a desk.

27. (**B**) What season is it?
  A. It is hot in summer.
  B. It is summer.
  C. It's Sunday.
  D. I like summer very much.

28. (**A**) Isn't there a washing machine in the house?

    A. Yes, there is.

    B. Yes, there is not.

    C. Please turn off the light.

    D. I do not mean it.

    * *washing machine* 洗衣機   mean〔min〕*v.* 有意

29. (**B**) How was your business yesterday?

    A. Everything was on sale.

    B. We didn't even sell a bun.

    C. We didn't have to pay anything.

    D. Our boss thought much about our customers.

    * bun〔bʌn〕*n.* 小圓麵包   *think much about* 很重視

30. (**C**) That's their new color TV.

    A. We can't wait!

    B. That's too bad.

    C. Really?　Why did they buy another TV?

    D. I wish it's ours.

    * (D)須改為 I wish it were ours.

Part C

31. (**A**) W: Bob, I need a new sweater.

    M: Why don't you pick one or two out and try them on?

    (TONE)

    Q: What does the man say to her?

    A. She should try on one or two sweaters.

    B. She must buy one or two sweaters.

    C. She should be ready to take two sweaters home.

    D. She should select one of the best sweaters.

    * *pick out* 挑選   *try on* 試穿

32. (**C**) M: Are you taking Professor Johnson's French 101 Course?
　　　　　　I heard it's a little tough.　How are you doing in it?
　　　　W: I can get along in that course, but I am not really fluent.

　　　　(TONE)
　　　　Q: What does the woman mean?
　　　　A. She doesn't know how she is doing in French.
　　　　B. Her four skills of French are highly improved.
　　　　C. Her speaking ability is average.
　　　　D. She can't manage the course as much as she wants to.

　　　　* tough〔tʌf〕*adj.* 困難的　　***get along*** 勉強應付　　***four skills*** 聽說讀寫

33. (**A**) W: Mr. Lee was born in Indonesia, wasn't he?
　　　　M: I don't know whether he was born there or not, but I've
　　　　　　heard him say he lived in Hong Kong when he was in
　　　　　　junior high.

　　　　(TONE)
　　　　Q: What doesn't the man know about Mr. Lee?
　　　　A. He doesn't know if Mr. Lee was born in Indonesia.
　　　　B. He doesn't know where Mr. Lee lived before.
　　　　C. He doesn't know when Mr. Lee will go to Hong Kong.
　　　　D. He doesn't know where Mr. Lee grew up.

34. (**B**) W: Could I borrow your geology book for a while?
　　　　M: You can if you can find it.

　　　　(TONE)
　　　　Q: What does the man mean?
　　　　A. He wants the woman to borrow his book.
　　　　B. He suggests that she find the book if she wants to borrow it.
　　　　C. If she had found the book, she could have.
　　　　D. He brought the book home, but it's disappeared.

　　　　* geology〔dʒɪˋalədʒɪ〕*n.* 地質學

35. (**B**) M: Now what's become of my fork?
　　　　　 W: There it is under your napkin.

　　　　　 (TONE)
　　　　　 Q: What is the man doing?
　　　　　 A. He is folding his napkin.
　　　　　 B. He is looking for his fork.
　　　　　 C. He is eating food without a fork.
　　　　　 D. He is becoming frustrated because he can't find his napkin.

　　　　　 * **become of** 變成；發生　　fork (fɔrk) n. 叉子
　　　　　 napkin ('næpkɪn) n. 餐巾

36. (**A**) W: What do you think of our new teacher?
　　　　　 M: We couldn't ask for a better teacher.

　　　　　 (TONE)
　　　　　 Q: What does the man mean?
　　　　　 A. He thinks she is an excellent teacher.
　　　　　 B. The new teacher is obnoxious.
　　　　　 C. There should be a better teacher than she.
　　　　　 D. She is a very rude teacher.

　　　　　 * obnoxious (əb'nɑkʃəs) adj. 令人討厭的　　rude (rud) adj. 粗魯的

37. (**B**) W: Shall we go to the concert?
　　　　　 M: No, not today. I have no money with me at all. Let's go
　　　　　　 to the rose garden for a change.

　　　　　 (TONE)
　　　　　 Q: Where will they go?
　　　　　 A. To the movies.
　　　　　 B. To the flower garden.
　　　　　 C. To the concert.
　　　　　 D. To the zoo.

38. (**C**)　W: If I order a sofa, could you send it today?
　　　　　M: I can have one of the boys deliver it this afternoon.

　　　　　(TONE)
　　　　　Q: What does the woman want the man to do?

　　　　　A. Order a sofa this afternoon.
　　　　　B. Send a catalog of sofas.
　　　　　C. Deliver a sofa.
　　　　　D. Sit on a sofa.

　　　　　* catalog ('kætl͵ɔg) *n.* 目錄

39. (**B**)　W: Don't you play golf any more?
　　　　　M: No, I've got a bad back.　I had to give that up.

　　　　　(TONE)
　　　　　Q: What's the man's problem?

　　　　　A. He can't swing a golf club well.
　　　　　B. He hurt his back.
　　　　　C. He used to be a good golfer, but is not any more.
　　　　　D. He always has a backache.

　　　　　* ***bad back*** 背痛　　swing (swɪŋ) *v.* 揮動
　　　　　golf club 高爾夫球桿　　golfer ('gɑlfə) *n.* 打高爾夫球的人
　　　　　backache ('bæk͵ek) *n.* 背痛

40. (**B**)　M: May I speak to Jason Daniels please?
　　　　　W: Nobody by that name works here.

　　　　　(TONE)
　　　　　Q: What does the woman mean?

　　　　　A. Jason Daniels isn't home right now.
　　　　　B. The man dialed the wrong number.
　　　　　C. Jason Daniels can't come to the phone right now.
　　　　　D. Jason Daniels doesn't want to speak to the caller.

41. (**B**) W: Do you drink a lot of coffee?

M: No, it's nice for a change, but I am a tea drinker myself.

(TONE)

Q: What does the man mean?

A. He is a coffee drinker.

B. He likes to drink tea.

C. He wants a coffee refill.

D. Coffee makes him sick.

* ***tea drinker*** 喜歡喝茶的人   refill (ri'fɪl) *n.* 續杯
sick (sɪk) *adj.* 噁心的

42. (**B**) M: How would you like to go to the cafeteria for dinner?

W: I don't mind going there, but if there is anything I hate it's standing in line.

(TONE)

Q: What does the woman say about dining at the cafeteria?

A. She feels that the man must go there by himself.

B. She is complaining about standing in line and waiting.

C. She is disappointed that the cafeteria is always crowded.

D. She feels she should stand in line.

* cafeteria (ˏkæfə'tɪrɪə) *n.* 自助餐廳   ***stand in line*** 排隊

43. (**B**) W: What a beautiful day it is! It's a perfect day for the football game.

M: Indeed, you couldn't ask for better weather.

(TONE)

Q: What does the man mean?

A. Everyone will enjoy the game today.

B. It's nice weather.

C. Tomorrow will be better weather.

D. He expected better weather.

44. (**C**) M: I eat three meals a day.　How about you?

W: I eat only once a day.　What really gets me is that you have never gained a pound.　How can you do that?

(TONE)

Q: What does the woman say about the man?

A. She feels that he should go on a diet.

B. She thinks that he must become a vegetarian.

C. She is surprised that he is not heavy.

D. She is upset that he is overweight.

* get (gɛt) v. 難倒　　vegetarian (ˌvɛdʒəˈtɛrɪən) n. 素食主義者
upset (ʌpˈsɛt) adj. 不高興的　　overweight (ˈovɚˌwet) n. 過重

45. (**B**) W: Oh, there's a spectacular view from here.　It's breathtaking.

M: Indeed.　Look, that river appears to run backward.

(TONE)

Q: What does the man say about the river?

A. The beautiful scene that he has never seen before is breathtaking.

B. The river appears to flow in the opposite direction.

C. The river starts from a lake.

D. The mountain range gives rise to many streams.

* spectacular (spɛkˈtækjəlɚ) adj. 壯觀的
breathtaking (ˈbrɛθˌtekɪŋ) adj. 令人興奮的；驚人的
mountain range 山脈　　*give rise to* 產生

Part D

46. (**C**) You've all heard of Walt Disney.　No one has ever delighted more children or adults than Walt Disney, the winner of 31 Academy Awards.　Almost everyone has heard of Mickey Mouse and Donald Duck, and his other popular characters like Minnie Mouse, Pluto, and Goofy.

(TONE)

Q: Which of the following Disney characters is not mentioned in this talk?

A. Donald Duck.
B. Pluto.
C. Snow White.
D. Goofy.

* *Academy Awards* 奧斯卡金像獎　character (ˈkærɪktɚ) *n.* 人物

47. (**C**) The park entrance will be closing in 15 minutes. Day visitors to Cimarron Canyon State Park should leave the park immediately. Guests in the campgrounds will still have full use of all facilities except canoes. Please put canoes and paddles on their racks. The entertainment program at the main lodge will begin in one hour.

(TONE)

Q: How long can the guests in the campgrounds stay in the park?

A. For 15 minutes.
B. For one hour.
C. All night long.
D. For two hours.

* canyon (ˈkænjən) *n.* 峽谷　campground (ˈkæmp͵graʊnd) *n.* 露營地
canoe (kəˈnu) *n.* 獨木舟　paddle (ˈpædl̩) *n.* 短槳
rack (ræk) *n.* 架子　*main lodge* (露營地的) 中心樓

48. (**B**) Good afternoon, folks. I'm sorry to tell you that today's showing of the movie *Scandals* is canceled because of a leak in the ceiling of the movie theater. We are sorry about this inconvenience. If you have already bought your tickets, your money will be refunded.

(TONE)

Q: What is the problem?

A. The tickets are all sold out.
B. The ceiling of the theater is leaking.
C. The movie is not very funny.
D. The film has been misplaced.

* folk (fok) *n.* 人　　cancel ('kænsl̩) *v.* 取消
  leak (lik) *n.* 漏水　　ceiling ('silɪŋ) *n.* 天花板
  refund (rɪ'fʌnd) *v.* 退錢　　misplace (mɪs'ples) *v.* 誤放；弄丟了

49. (**B**) When you order a la carte dishes, you pay a separate price for each item on the menu.　A la carte is opposed to table d'hote. The latter is a regular dinner.　It is a complete meal which has courses as specified on the menu and which is served for a set price.

(TONE)

Q: What is the opposite of a la carte?

A. A menu.
B. A set-price dinner.
C. A table.
D. A dessert.

* a la carte (ˌɑlə'kɑrt) *n.* 單點的菜
  table d'hote ('tebl̩'dot) *n.* 套餐；和菜
  course (kɔrs) *n.* 一道菜　　specify ('spɛsəˌfaɪ) *v.* 指定
  set (sɛt) *adj.* 固定的　　dessert (dɪ'zɝt) *n.* 甜點

50. (**C**) Over the years, balloonists tried unsuccessfully to cross the Atlantic Ocean.　It wasn't until 1978 that three American balloonists succeeded.　It took them just six days to make the trip from their home in the United States to Paris, France.

(TONE)

Q: How long did the Atlantic flight take?

A. One day.   B. Three days.

C. Six days.   D. Eleven days.

* balloonist (bə'lunɪst) *n.* 氣球飛行器駕駛員   flight (flaɪt) *n.* 飛行

51. (**B**) Whenever journalists face a news famine, they revive the undeniably interesting question. How can we explain UFOs — unidentified flying objects? Newspaper editors like these stories because they keep the population interested in knowledge about UFOs and keep them buying newspapers.

(TONE)

Q: Why do newspaper editors love the stories about UFOs?

A. They make exciting writing.

B. They help to sell papers.

C. People hate to read these articles.

D. UFOs are rare stories.

* journalist ('dʒɝnḷɪst) *n.* 記者   famine ('fæmɪn) *n.* 極度缺乏；饑荒
revive (rɪ'vaɪv) *v.* 使復活
undeniably (ˌʌnˌdɪ'naɪəblɪ) *adv.* 不可否認地
unidentified (ˌʌnˌaɪ'dɛntəˌfaɪd) *adj.* 不明的   rare (rɛr) *adj.* 罕見的

52. (**B**) I think I've covered neurocontrol of voluntary actions. Now I'd like to continue today's lecture with a discussion about the functioning of nerves in involuntary actions.

(TONE)

Q: Who is the speaker?

A. A pupil.   B. A biology professor.

C. An eye specialist.   D. A safety expert.

* cover ('kʌvɚ) *v.* (範圍) 包含
neurocontrol (ˌnjurokən'trol) *n.* 神經控制
voluntary actions 自主行動   *involuntary actions* 不自主行動
pupil ('pjupḷ) *n.* 學生   *eye specialist* 眼科醫師

53. (**C**) Taiwan's rapidly aging population will reach a critical point in 2007, a spokesman for the Taipei Health Institute said yesterday. The number of people in Taiwan aged 65 and older will comprise 20 percent in 2007.

(TONE)
Q: What percentage of the population is over age 65 now?
A. 20.
B. More than 20.
C. Less than 20.
D. 7.

* aging ('edʒɪŋ) adj. 老化的   *critical point* 臨界點
  spokesman ('spoksmən) n. 發言人
  comprise (kəm'praɪz) v. 組成

54. (**C**) Paging Ms. Lily Williamson. Please report to the Lost and Found Center.

(TONE)
Q: What is the purpose of this announcement?
A. To help Ms. Williamson find the Lost and Found Center.
B. To tell Ms. Williamson that she has a telephone call.
C. To bring Ms. Williamson to the Lost and Found Center.
D. To report that Ms. Williamson is lost.

* page (pedʒ) v. 呼名找人
  the Lost and Found Center 失物招領中心

55. (**C**) Train number 23 bound for New York has been delayed 40 minutes. The track number has also been changed to 7. Dinner will be available on board. You'll also be able to buy alcoholic beverages.

(TONE)

Q: What is this announcement for?

A. A flight schedule.

B. Dinner in a restaurant.

C. A train.

D. A bus.

* **be bound for** 前往   track ﹝træk﹞ *n.* 軌道
   on board 在火車上   beverage ﹝'bɛvɪrɪdʒ﹞ *n.* 飲料

56. (**A**) The main item on our agenda is our contract with National Express as our courier service.　NatEx is willing to make slight reductions but not what other companies are offering.

(TONE)

Q: Where would this be heard?

A. At a board of directors meeting.

B. At a courier service counter.

C. At a contract signing ceremony.

D. At a funeral ceremony.

* agenda ﹝ə'dʒɛndə﹞ *n.* 議程；討論事項
  express ﹝ɪks'prɛs﹞ *n.* 快遞
  courier ﹝'kʊrɪə﹞ *n.* 信使   **board of directors** 董事會
  contract ﹝'kɑntrækt﹞ *n.* 合約   funeral ﹝'fjunərəl﹞ *n.* 葬禮

57. (**B**) Listen to CVBC and get all the news your life calls for 24 hours a day.　Only CVBC is all news all the time with new reports phoned in hourly.　Whether it's weather, sports, business, local, provincial or international news, CVBC has all the news Taipei needs.

(TONE)

Q: What is this commercial advertising?

A. A newspaper.

B. A radio station.

C. A telephone company.

D. A magazine.

　* local (ˈlokl̩) *adj.* 本地的　　provincial (prəˈvɪnʃəl) *adj.* 全省的
　commercial (kəˈmɝʃəl) *n.* 商業廣告

58. (**C**) I suggest that there is an easy way to solve the housing
　　problem we are facing.　Let's move the state legislature
　　into tents and let needy families move into the Capitol.
　　At least that way we might get something for our tax money.

(TONE)

Q: What is the main purpose of the speaker?

A. He is trying to make a serious proposal.

B. He is trying to ask for information.

C. He is trying to amuse the audience.

D. He is trying to warn the audience.

　* legislature (ˈlɛdʒɪsˌletʃɚ) *n.* 立法院；議會　　needy (ˈnidɪ) *adj.* 貧窮的
　Capitol (ˈkæpɪtəl) *n.* 州議會議廳　　amuse (əˈmjuz) *v.* 使娛樂

59. (**C**) Come to the opening of the Organic Vegetable Market!
　　Someday soon, such an advertisement might be a reality.　On
　　November 13, there will be a meeting at Medford High describing
　　the benefits of making your operations organic.

(TONE)

Q: Who is this commercial aimed at?

A. Consumers.　　　　　B. Doctors.

C. Farmers.　　　　　　D. Students.

　* organic (ɔrˈgænɪk) *adj.* 有機的
　operation (ˌɑpəˈreʃən) *n.* 企業；工作　　***be aimed at*** 針對

60. (**A**) Ladies and gentlemen, may I have your attention please. There will be three animal shows this afternoon at the City Zoo. The first show will begin at three o'clock in the marine arena. There, Flipper the dolphin and Orca the killer whale will dazzle the audience with jumps and flips and other funny antics.

(TONE)

Q: What is the purpose of this announcement?

A. To inform people of the zoo show.

B. To announce the zoo will close soon.

C. To advertise goods sold at the gift shop.

D. To promote a restaurant serving lunch at the zoo.

* marine〔mə'rin〕*adj.* 海洋的　　arena〔ə'rinə〕*n.* 競技場；場地
flipper〔'flɪpɚ〕*n.* 鰭狀肢　　dolphin〔'dɑlfɪn〕*n.* 海豚
killer whale 殺人鯨　　dazzle〔'dæzl̩〕*v.* 使讚嘆不已
flip〔flɪp〕*n.* 空翻　　antic〔'æntɪk〕*n.* 滑稽的動作

English Listening Comprehension Test

Test Book No. 7

This listening comprehension test will test your ability to understand spoken English. In this test, each conversation, statement and question will be spoken JUST ONE TIME. They will not be written out for you. There are four parts to this test. Special instructions will be given to you at the beginning of each part.

Part A

In Part A, you will see several pictures in your test book. For each picture, you will be asked 1 to 3 questions. For each question, you will hear four possible answers. Choose the best answer according to what you see in the picture.

Example:

You will see:

You will hear: What is this?
A. This is a table.
B. This is a chair.
C. This is a watch.
D. This is a doll.

The best answer to the question "What is this?" is B: "This is a chair." Therefore, you should choose answer B.

A. <u>Questions 1-2</u>

D. <u>Questions 9-10</u>

B. <u>Questions 3-5</u>

E. <u>Questions 11-12</u>

C. <u>Questions 6-8</u>

F. <u>Questions 13-15</u>

Part B

In Part B, you will hear 15 questions.   After you hear a question, read the four possible answers in your test book and decide which one is the best answer to the question you have heard.

Example:

<u>You will hear:</u>   What does your father do?

<u>You will read:</u>   A. He's 50 years old.
　　　　　　　　　B. He's a teacher.
　　　　　　　　　C. He's hungry.
　　　　　　　　　D. He's in Los Angeles.

The best answer to the question "What does your father do?" is B: "He's a teacher."   Therefore, you should choose answer B.

Please go to the next page. ⟹

16. A. That is a good idea.
    B. I have many swimsuits.
    C. I have no idea.
    D. When will you go?

17. A. I am sorry. He is not
       at home now.
    B. Who are you?
    C. Mr. Lin can speak good
       English.
    D. What do you mean?

18. A. He is in the living room.
    B. He is not in the room.
    C. He is watching TV.
    D. He is studying.

19. A. By bus.
    B. I liked it.
    C. I had a present.
    D. Many people were there.

20. A. Of course, but I can't.
    B. Yes, I have a math test.
    C. All right, you don't.
    D. Yes, I don't want to.

21. A. So did I.
    B. Neither did I.
    C. So I did.
    D. Neither I did.

22. A. That's okay.
    B. That's a good idea.
    C. What are you saying?
    D. No, I guess not.

23. A. Yes, I have. I have
       borrowed one.
    B. Yes, I do. I have
       borrowed one.
    C. Yes, you are. I have
       borrowed one.
    D. Yes, I have. I have lent
       one.

24. A. I have many neighbors.
    B. I am glad to meet you.
    C. My neighbors all live
       here.
    D. It sounds interesting.

25. A. She is a teacher.
    B. She is my aunt.
    C. She swims in the pool.
    D. She goes to the park every
       day.

26. A. A deal is a deal.
    B. So will you.
    C. What can I do?
    D. I hope so.

27. A. Yes, I didn't turn it on.
    B. No, and I'll turn it on
       yesterday.
    C. No, but I'll turn it on right
       away.
    D. Yes, I'll turn it on right
       away.

28. A. Yes, I'm right.
    B. Yes, something happened.
    C. No, I happened to
       something.
    D. No, there's something
       wrong with me.

29. A. Yesterday was a nice day.
    B. Yesterday was October 5.
    C. It rained yesterday.
    D. Yesterday was Thursday.

30. A. Yes, I did need help.
    B. No, you may.
    C. Yes, I want some shirts.
    D. Why?

Part C

In Part C, you will hear 15 conversations between a man and a woman. After each conversation, you will hear a question about the conversation. After you hear the question, read the four possible answers in your test book and choose the best answer to the question you have heard.

Example:

<u>You will hear:</u> (Man)   How do you go to school every day?
(Woman) Usually by bus. Sometimes by taxi.

TONE: How does the woman go to school?

<u>You will read:</u> A. She always goes to school on foot.
B. She usually takes a bike.
C. She takes either a bus or a taxi.
D. She usually goes to school by bus, never by taxi.

The best answer to the question "How does the woman go to school?" is C: "She takes either a bus or a taxi." Therefore, you should choose answer C.

Please go to the next page. ⟹

31. A. Cleaning the house on
    Monday.
    B. Putting things away in his
    office on Monday.
    C. His health problem.
    D. The weather on Monday.

32. A. Where he can get a good
    car.
    B. How often he can travel
    by his car.
    C. How much he can sell his
    car for.
    D. Whether or not he can
    drive to California and
    come back.

33. A. He was tired.
    B. His appointment was
    changed.
    C. He had a flat tire.
    D. His bicycle was stolen.

34. A. Check-in counter at the
    airport.
    B. At the gate at the airport.
    C. In the air.
    D. At customs.

35. A. He will be ready for take
    off.
    B. He will be ready to board.
    C. He will arrive in Colorado.
    D. He will stow all luggage
    under the seat.

36. A. She is teaching a different
    subject.
    B. She was dismissed.
    C. She is changing jobs.
    D. She doesn't like teaching
    any more.

37. A. She's afraid of going out
    at night.
    B. She had to do some baking.
    C. She wanted to get ready
    for a plane trip.
    D. She was moving to a new
    apartment.

38. A. Shave.
    B. Finish with green paint.
    C. Move in here.
    D. Travel.

39. A. To see the Dean.
 B. To watch the team.
 C. To weigh herself.
 D. To give a demonstration.

40. A. Near an art gallery.
 B. In front of a library.
 C. At a stoplight.
 D. Outside a bookstore.

41. A. His change.
 B. Something to read.
 C. A different waitress.
 D. A copy of the order form.

42. A. Take his typewriter to the
    repair shop.
 B. Soundproof his room.
 C. Work in the basement.
 D. Listen for his roommate.

43. A. They work in the same
    department.
 B. They are distantly related.
 C. They are both doctors.
 D. They are both chemists.

44. A. He's better.
 B. He's complaining.
 C. He's sick in bed.
 D. He's cold.

45. A. Try on the jacket.
 B. Try on the suit.
 C. Continue looking.
 D. Buy a fur coat.

Part D

In Part D, you will hear 15 short talks. After each talk, you will hear a question about the talk. After you hear the question, read the four possible answers in your test book and choose the best answer to the question you have heard.

Example:

<u>You will hear:</u> Well, that's all for Unit 15. For today's homework, please do the review questions on page 80, and we'll check the answers tomorrow. Now, let's go on to Unit 16.

TONE: What is the teacher going to do next in today's class?

<u>You will read:</u> A. Check the homework.
B. Review Unit 15.
C. Start a new unit.
D. Answer students' questions.

The best answer to the question "What is the teacher going to do next in today's class?" is C: "Start a new unit." Therefore, you should choose answer C.

Please go to the next page. ⇨

46. A. To demonstrate tutoring techniques.
    B. To explain school policies.
    C. To recruit workers.
    D. To explain a service.

47. A. He'll work at Silverlode.
    B. He'll fire Mr. Haskell.
    C. He'll ask Mr. Haskell again.
    D. He'll stay on as president.

48. A. Sunday.
    B. Tuesday.
    C. Friday.
    D. Saturday.

49. A. Five.
    B. Six.
    C. Seven.
    D. Eight.

50. A. Film and society.
    B. A film society.
    C. Rare films.
    D. How to make a film.

51. A. Synthetic materials.
    B. Masses of seaweed.
    C. Parts of vegetables.
    D. Parts of animals and fish.

52. A. A dog.
    B. A musical instrument.
    C. A ship.
    D. A horse.

53. A. Cartoons.
    B. The rural Mid-west.
    C. His father.
    D. Traveling around the world.

54. A. Stones.
    B. Hands.
    C. A hat.
    D. A scarf.

55. A. Experienced drivers.
    B. New drivers.
    C. Driving examiners.
    D. Movie-goers.

56. A. Discussing psychology.
    B. Introducing a speaker.
    C. Murdering someone.
    D. Solving a crime.

57. A. Question the offer.
    B. Reject the offer.
    C. Begin a strike.
    D. Accept the offer.

58. A. That the flight is boarding.
    B. That a caller is waiting.
    C. That Dr. Reed should
       make a phone call.
    D. That the line is busy.

59. A. A lower drinking age.
    B. Cutting cedar trees.
    C. Shortage of water.
    D. The cost of beer.

60. A. The date when the first
       exam will take place.
    B. The date when the school
       will begin.
    C. The date when the paper
       is due.
    D. The date when the
       instructor left.

Listening Test 7 詳解

Part A

For questions number 1 to 2, please look at picture A.

1. (**B**) Question number 1, what is the man on the right doing?
   A. He is pointing and writing.
   B. He is shouting and pointing.
   C. He is writing.
   D. He is whispering.

2. (**D**) Question number 2, please look at picture A again. Who is the man on the left?
   A. He is a salesman.
   B. He is a flight attendant.
   C. He is a reporter.
   D. He is a police officer.

   * *flight attendant* 空服員

For questions number 3 to 5, please look at picture B.

3. (**B**) Question number 3, what is the family doing?
   A. The family is cooking.
   B. The family is toasting each other.
   C. The family is watching TV.
   D. The family is ordering food.

   * toast〔tost〕v. 敬酒

4. (**D**) Question number 4, please look at picture B again. What are they eating?
   A. They are eating Italian food.
   B. They are eating American food.
   C. They are eating Indian food.
   D. They are eating Chinese food.

5. (**B**) Question number 5, please look at picture B again. What are they going to eat with?

    A. They are going to eat with their fingers.

    B. They are going to eat with chopsticks.

    C. They are going to eat with knives.

    D. They are going to eat with forks.

    * chopsticks ('tʃɑp‚stɪks) *n.pl.* 筷子

For questions number 6 to 8, please look at picture C.

6. (**B**) Question number 6, how many people are there in this family?

    A. Three.

    B. Five.

    C. Two.

    D. Six.

7. (**C**) Question number 7, please look at picture C again. Where is the father sitting?

    A. The father is sitting on a desk.

    B. The father is sitting on a sofa.

    C. The father is sitting on an armchair.

    D. The father is sitting on the floor.

    * armchair ('ɑrm‚tʃɛr) *n.* 有扶手的椅子

8. (**B**) Question number 8, please look at picture C again. What is the little daughter doing?

    A. She is writing.

    B. She is playing with a cat.

    C. She is reading.

    D. She is painting.

For questions number 9 to 10, please look at picture D.

9. (**C**) Question number 9, who is the man in the middle?

    A. He is a soldier.

    B. He is a mechanic.

    C. He is a graduate.

    D. He is a gardener.

    * mechanic (məˈkænɪk) *n.* 技師   graduate (ˈgrædʒuɪt) *n.* 畢業生
gardener (ˈgɑrdṇɚ) *n.* 園丁

10. (**C**) Question number 10, please look at picture D again.　What is he holding?

    A. He is holding a magazine.

    B. He is holding a hat.

    C. He is holding a diploma.

    D. He is holding a pair of glasses.

    * diploma (dɪˈplomə) *n.* 畢業證書

For questions number 11 to 12, please look at picture E.

11. (**C**) Question number 11, what is lady "A" doing?

    A. She is pushing a box.

    B. She is pulling a car.

    C. She is pushing a shopping cart.

    D. She is pulling a shopping bag.

    * *shopping cart* （購物）手推車

12. (**B**) Question number 12, please look at picture E again.　Where is the man "B"?

    A. He is standing behind a safe.

    B. He is standing behind a cash register.

    C. He is standing behind a bank.

    D. He is standing behind an ATM.

    * safe (sef) *n.* 保險箱   *cash register* 收銀機
ATM 自動提款機 (= *automatic teller machine*)

For questions number 13 to 15, please look at picture F.

13. (**C**) Question number 13, where is the man?
  A. He is in the living room.
  B. He is in the kitchen.
  C. He is in the bedroom.
  D. He is in the bathroom.

14. (**D**) Question number 14, please look at picture F again.　What is
  the man holding?
  A. He is holding a hat.
  B. He is holding a cup of coffee.
  C. He is holding an umbrella.
  D. He is holding a pillow.
  * pillow ('pɪlo) *n.* 枕頭

15. (**C**) Question number 15, please look at picture F again.　Where is
  the lamp?
  A. It is on the dresser.
  B. It is on the cupboard.
  C. It is on the night table.
  D. It is on the bed.
  * dresser ('drɛsɚ) *n.* 梳妝台　　cupboard ('kʌbɚd) *n.* 碗櫥
  night table 床頭櫃

Part B

16. (**A**) Let's go swimming.
  A. That is a good idea.
  B. I have many swimsuits.
  C. I have no idea.
  D. When will you go?

17. (**A**) Hello, may I speak to Mr. Lin?
    A. I am sorry. He is not at home now.
    B. Who are you?
    C. Mr. Lin can speak good English.
    D. What do you mean?

18. (**A**) Where is your father?
    A. He is in the living room.
    B. He is not in the room.
    C. He is watching TV.
    D. He is studying.

19. (**A**) How did you go to the party?
    A. By bus.
    B. I liked it.
    C. I had a present.
    D. Many people were there.

20. (**A**) Don't you want to watch TV tonight?
    A. Of course, but I can't.
    B. Yes, I have a math test.
    C. All right, you don't.
    D. Yes, I don't want to.

21. (**B**) I bought some bread, but I didn't buy any fruit.
    A. So did I.
    B. Neither did I.
    C. So I did.
    D. Neither I did.

22. (**D**) Is there any other thing I can do for you?
    A. That's okay.
    B. That's a good idea.
    C. What are you saying?
    D. No, I guess not.

23. (**A**) Have you prepared your sleeping-bag?
   A. Yes, I have. I have borrowed one.
   B. Yes, I do. I have borrowed one.
   C. Yes, you are. I have borrowed one.
   D. Yes, I have. I have lent one.
   * ***sleeping-bag*** 睡袋

24. (**B**) Hi, my name is John. I am your neighbor.
   A. I have many neighbors.
   B. I am glad to meet you.
   C. My neighbors all live here.
   D. It sounds interesting.

25. (**A**) What kind of work does Miss Li do?
   A. She is a teacher.
   B. She is my aunt.
   C. She swims in the pool.
   D. She goes to the park every day.

26. (**D**) We will have a lot of fun camping in the mountains.
   A. A deal is a deal.
   B. So will you.
   C. What can I do?
   D. I hope so.
   * ***A deal is a deal***. 一言爲定。

27. (**C**) Did you turn on the light?
   A. Yes, I didn't turn it on.
   B. No, and I'll turn it on yesterday.
   C. No, but I'll turn it on right away.
   D. Yes, I'll turn it on right away.

28. (**D**)　Are you all right, Steve?
　　　　A. Yes, I'm right.
　　　　B. Yes, something happened.
　　　　C. No, I happened to something.
　　　　D. No, there's something wrong with me.

29. (**D**)　Today is Friday.　What day was yesterday?
　　　　A. Yesterday was a nice day.
　　　　B. Yesterday was October 5.
　　　　C. It rained yesterday.
　　　　D. Yesterday was Thursday.

30. (**C**)　May I help you, sir?
　　　　A. Yes, I did need help.
　　　　B. No, you may.
　　　　C. Yes, I want some shirts.
　　　　D. Why?

Part C

31. (**D**)　W: Did he say it was going to clear up Monday?
　　　　M: He didn't say, but it probably will.

　　　　(TONE)
　　　　Q: What are they talking about?
　　　　A. Cleaning the house on Monday.
　　　　B. Putting things away in his office on Monday.
　　　　C. His health problem.
　　　　D. The weather on Monday.
　　　　* **clear up** （天氣）放晴

32. (**D**)　W: George, do you think your old car is going to make it to
　　　　　　California and back?
　　　　M: No problem.

(TONE)

Q: What is the woman worrying about?

A. Where he can get a good car.

B. How often he can travel by his car.

C. How much he can sell his car for.

D. Whether or not he can drive to California and come back.

* make it 成功；做到

33. (**C**) W: Why are you so late?　I've been waiting for more than half an hour.

M: My bicycle had a flat tire, and I had to walk.

(TONE)

Q: Why was the man late?

A. He was tired.

B. His appointment was changed.

C. He had a flat tire.

D. His bicycle was stolen.

34. (**A**) M: Do you have any luggage to check through?

W: Yes, this one suitcase.

(TONE)

Q: Where does this conversation take place?

A. Check-in counter at the airport.

B. At the gate at the airport.

C. In the air.

D. At customs.

* check (tʃɛk) v. 託運　　suitcase ('sut͵kes) n. 行李箱
  check-in counter （航空公司）辦理登機手續的櫃台
  customs ('kʌstəmz) n. 海關

35. (**C**)　M: How long will it be before we're in Colorado?
　　　　　W: We expect to be on the ground in about fifteen minutes.

　　　　　(TONE)
　　　　　Q: What will the man do in fifteen minutes?
　　　　　A. He will be ready for take off.
　　　　　B. He will be ready to board.
　　　　　C. He will arrive in Colorado.
　　　　　D. He will stow all luggage under the seat.
　　　　　*** on the ground** 著陸　　board〔bord〕v. 登機　　stow〔sto〕v. 放入

36. (**B**)　M: Nancy, why isn't Dr. Johnson teaching here this semester?
　　　　　W: She was fired.

　　　　　(TONE)
　　　　　Q: Why isn't Dr. Johnson teaching?
　　　　　A. She is teaching a different subject.
　　　　　B. She was dismissed.
　　　　　C. She is changing jobs.
　　　　　D. She doesn't like teaching any more.
　　　　　* dismiss〔dɪs'mɪs〕v. 解雇

37. (**C**)　M: How about going to dinner and a movie with me tonight,
　　　　　　　Sandy?
　　　　　W: I'd love to, but I haven't packed yet, and my flight leaves
　　　　　　　at five A.M.

　　　　　(TONE)
　　　　　Q: Why didn't Sandy accept the invitation?
　　　　　A. She's afraid of going out at night.
　　　　　B. She had to do some baking.
　　　　　C. She wanted to get ready for a plane trip.
　　　　　D. She was moving to a new apartment.

38. (**D**) W: I heard that you're planning a trip for next summer, Jim.
      M: I hope to tour Italy if I finish my degree in time and save
           enough money.

      (TONE)
      Q: What does Jim plan to do?
      A. Shave.
      B. Finish with green paint.
      C. Move in here.
      D. Travel.

39. (**A**) M: Can you tell me where the Dean's office is?
      W: I'm on my way there myself, so I'll show you.

      (TONE)
      Q: Where is the woman going?
      A. To see the Dean.
      B. To watch the team.
      C. To weigh herself.
      D. To give a demonstration.

      * dean (din) *n.* 院長；系主任；教務長
        demonstration (ˌdɛmən'streʃən) *n.* 示威；示範

40. (**D**) M: Stop for a minute. I want to look at this display in the
           window.
      W: I see some books are on sale. Let's go inside and see if
           we can find something on art.

      (TONE)
      Q: Where are they standing?
      A. Near an art gallery.
      B. In front of a library.
      C. At a stoplight.
      D. Outside a bookstore.

      * *art gallery* 藝廊   stoplight ('stɑpˌlaɪt) *n.* 紅燈

41. (**A**) W: Are you ready to order now?
        M: No, I just finished. I'm waiting for my change.

        (TONE)
        Q: What does the man want?
        A. His change.
        B. Something to read.
        C. A different waitress.
        D. A copy of the order form.

42. (**C**) M: I have to type my paper later tonight, but I'm afraid my
             roommate won't be able to sleep.
        W: There's a sound-proof typing room in the basement.
            You can take your typewriter down there, and no one
            will hear it.

        (TONE)
        Q: What will the man probably do to avoid disturbing his
           roommate?
        A. Take his typewriter to the repair shop.
        B. Soundproof his room.
        C. Work in the basement.
        D. Listen for his roommate.
        * sound-proof ('saund,pruf) adj. 隔音的
          basement ('besmənt) n. 地下室　　disturb (dɪ'stɝb) v. 打擾

43. (**D**) W: Tom, I'd like you to meet my sister Sara Johnson. Sara is
            also a chemist.
        M: It's nice to meet you, Sara. I believe we even work for
            the same drug company although in different departments.

(TONE)

Q: What do Tom and Sara have in common?

A. They work in the same department.

B. They are distantly related.

C. They are both doctors.

D. They are both chemists.

> * chemist ('kɛmɪst) *n.* 化學家；藥劑師
> department (dɪ'pɑrtmənt) *n.* 部門
> ***have in common*** 有共同點　　***be distantly related*** 是遠親

44. (**A**) W: I heard you caught a cold.　How are you doing today?
　　　　M: I can't complain.　At least I'm not in bed.

(TONE)

Q: How is the man today?

A. He's better.

B. He's complaining.

C. He's sick in bed.

D. He's cold.

45. (**C**) M: Would you like to try on that jacket, Madam?
　　　　W: Thank you, but I think I'll look further.　That color doesn't
　　　　　　suit me.

(TONE)

Q: What will the customer do next?

A. Try on the jacket.

B. Try on the suit.

C. Continue looking.

D. Buy a fur coat.

> * further ('fɜ˞ðə˞) *adv.* 再度；進一步地　　fur (fɜ˞) *n.* 毛皮

Part D

46. (**D**) At this university we offer two different programs for students who have children. For those of you with very young children, we have a day care program that takes infants from 3 months to 30 months. We have another program for children between two and five years of age.

(TONE)
Q: What is the main purpose of this announcement?
A. To demonstrate tutoring techniques.
B. To explain school policies.
C. To recruit workers.
D. To explain a service.

* infant ('ɪnfənt) n. 嬰兒   demonstrate ('dɛmən,stret) v. 示範
tutor ('tutɚ) v. 教學   recruit (rɪ'krut) v. 招募 (新人)

47. (**D**) I planned to announce Bob Haskell as Komcore's next president. I was quite surprised when Mr. Haskell rejected my offer and, instead, announced his departure to go work for Silverlode, our greatest competitor. This is a great threat to our company. I will, therefore, stay on for at least the next two years.

(TONE)
Q: What will the president do?
A. He'll work at Silverlode.
B. He'll fire Mr. Haskell.
C. He'll ask Mr. Haskell again.
D. He'll stay on as president.

* reject (rɪ'dʒɛkt) v. 拒絕   departure (dɪ'pɑrtʃɚ) n. 離職
competitor (kəm'pɛpətɚ) n. 競爭者;對手   *stay on* 留任

48. (**D**) Our first class will be held on the fieldhouse lawn this Saturday. If it rains, it will be held in the gym. You should wear athletic clothes and sport shoes. After this first Saturday, classes will be held every other Saturday.

(TONE)

Q: On what day of the week is the event to be held?

A. Sunday.
B. Tuesday.
C. Friday.
D. Saturday.

* fieldhouse ('fild,haus) *n.* 體育館　　lawn (lɔn) *n.* 草地
gym (dʒɪm) *n.* 體育館　　*athletic clothes* 運動服

49. (**B**) To make certain that you have read the assignments, I will give you a short unannounced quiz from time to time. This class meets on Mondays, Wednesdays, and Fridays. You will have a total of six major tests throughout the semester.

(TONE)

Q: How many tests will the students have throughout the semester?

A. Five.
B. Six.
C. Seven.
D. Eight.

* unannounced (,ʌnə'naunst) *adj.* 未經宣布的；突然的
quiz (kwɪz) *n.* 小考

50. (**B**) I belong to a small film society which meets once a month at our village hall. There are about 40 members, all of whom are keen film fans and most of whom know a great deal about the history of the cinema. The film society gives us the opportunity to see old and rare films which are seldom shown.

(TONE)
Q: What is the speaker discussing?
A. Film and society.　　B. A film society.
C. Rare films.　　D. How to make a film.

* society (sə'saɪətɪ) *n.* 社團　　hall (hɔl) *n.* 大會堂
keen (kin) *adj.* 熱切的　　cinema ('sɪnəmə) *n.* 電影

51. (**D**) There are three basic materials from which true glues are
made: animal bones, animal skins and fish heads.　Heating
these materials in water breaks down the component protein
called collagen.

(TONE)
Q: What are true glues made from?
A. Synthetic materials.
B. Masses of seaweed.
C. Parts of vegetables.
D. Parts of animals and fish.

* glue (glu) *n.* 漿糊；膠　　heat (hit) *v.* 加熱
break down 分解　　component (kəm'ponənt) *adj.* 組成的
protein ('protiɪn) *n.* 蛋白質　　collagen ('kɑlədʒɪn) *n.* 膠原蛋白
synthetic (sɪn'θɛtɪk) *adj.* 人工合成的　　mass (mæs) *n.* 團；塊

52. (**C**) When Charles Darwin sailed in the ship the Beagle in 1831, an
epic voyage of science had begun.　The marvelous variety of
life he saw intrigued him, filling his mind and his notebooks.

(TONE)
Q: What was the Beagle?
A. A dog.
B. A musical instrument.
C. A ship.
D. A horse.

* beagle ('bigḷ) *n.* 畢哥獵犬　　epic ('ɛpɪk) *adj.* 史詩般的；雄壯的
voyage ('vɔɪ·ɪdʒ) *n.* 旅程　　intrigue (ɪn'trig) *v.* 激起～的好奇心
musical instrument 樂器

53. (**B**) Walt Disney was the son of a Missouri farmer.　Around him was a world of animals on which many of his cartoons and films were based.　Disney was strongly influenced by the rural Mid-west where he grew up.

(TONE)

Q: What influenced Disney?

A. Cartoons.

B. The rural Mid-west.

C. His father.

D. Traveling around the world.

* rural (ˈrʊrəl) *adj.* 鄉村的

54. (**B**) In all places where there is snow, children roll big balls of snow to make snowmen.　They usually decorate a snowman with stones and use perhaps a carrot for his nose and an old hat and scarf for his head.

(TONE)

Q: What is not mentioned as decoration for a snowman?

A. Stones.　　　　　B. Hands.

C. A hat.　　　　　D. A scarf.

* roll (rol) *v.* 滾　　carrot (ˈkærət) *n.* 紅蘿蔔

55. (**A**) To renew licenses, apply at Window Two.　Complete the written test and return it to the window before you pick up your new license.

(TONE)

Q: Who is this announcement for?

A. Experienced drivers.

B. New drivers.

C. Driving examiners.

D. Movie-goers.

* renew (rɪˈnju) *v.* 更新　　apply (əˈplaɪ) *v.* 申請
examiner (ɪgˈzæmənɚ) *n.* 考官

56. (**B**) Ladies and Gentlemen: Today's guest speaker is the famous expert on Criminology from London who has established himself as the "sleuth" of the century. He has solved thousands of homicides and written several books on the criminal mind.

(TONE)

Q: What is the speaker doing?

A. Discussing psychology.
B. Introducing a speaker.
C. Murdering someone.
D. Solving a crime.

* criminology (͵krɪmə'nɑlətɪ) n. 犯罪學　　sleuth (sluθ) n. 偵探
homicide ('hɑmə͵saɪd) n. 殺人　　*criminal mind* 犯罪心理

57. (**D**) Today, you're voting on the negotiated settlement. We hoped to get a raise of at least $ 1.00, but the best they could do was $ .75. If this is not enough, the strike will go on. But, all of us are losing income. I, therefore, give this agreement my qualified endorsement.

(TONE)

Q: What are the members asked to do?

A. Question the offer.
B. Reject the offer.
C. Begin a strike.
D. Accept the offer.

* vote (vot) v. 投票　　negotiated (nɪ'goʃɪ͵etɪd) adj. 談判過的
settlement ('sɛtḷmənt) n. 協議　　raise (rez) n. 加薪
strike (straɪk) n. 罷工　　agreement (ə'grimənt) n. 協議
qualified ('kwɑlə͵faɪd) adj. 有條件的
endorsement (ɪn'dɔrsmənt) n. 背書；贊成
question ('kwɛstʃən) v. 質疑

58. (**B**) Would Dr. Thomas Reed please pick up the nearest courtesy phone? You have an urgent, long-distance call. Courtesy phones are marked in yellow and can be seen on the outer walls of the terminal. Simply identify yourself and the operator will connect you to your call.

(TONE)

Q: What does the message mean?

A. That the flight is boarding.

B. That a caller is waiting.

C. That Dr. Reed should make a phone call.

D. That the line is busy.

* courtesy ('kɝtəsɪ) *n.* 禮貌　*adj.* 免費的
  courtesy phone 免付費電話
  urgent ('ɝdʒənt) *adj.* 緊急的　***long-distance call*** 長途電話
  terminal ('tɝmənl) *n.* (公車、火車) 總站；航空站
  identify (aɪ'dɛntə,faɪ) *v.* 表明身分　connect (kə'nɛkt) *v.* 接通

59. (**C**) Last month's warmer weather increased demand for beer. Masterson Brewery, however, cut production. The warmer weather lowered the Cedar River. Water had to be diverted from the brewery for drinking water.

(TONE)

Q: What made the company's production change?

A. A lower drinking age.

B. Cutting cedar trees.

C. Shortage of water.

D. The cost of beer.

* demand (dɪ'mænd) *n.* 需求
  brewery ('bruərɪ) *n.* 釀酒廠；啤酒廠
  divert (də'vɝt) *v.* 轉向　cedar ('sidɚ) *n.* 西洋杉
  shortage ('ʃɔrtɪdʒ) *n.* 缺乏

60. (**C**) Good morning. My name is John Smith, and I will be the main instructor for this semester's history class. In this class, there will be three midterms and one final exam at the end of the semester. In addition, there will be one paper that is due on January 15th, at the end of this school term.

(TONE)

Q: What is the significance of January 15th?

A. The date when the first exam will take place.

B. The date when the school will begin.

C. The date when the paper is due.

D. The date when the instructor left.

* instructor (ɪn'strʌktɚ) *n.* 指導者；老師
midterm ('mɪd,tɝm) *n.* 期中考　　due (dju) *adj.* 到期的
significance (sɪg'nɪfəkəns) *n.* 重要性

English Listening Comprehension Test

Test Book No. 8

This listening comprehension test will test your ability to understand spoken English. In this test, each conversation, statement and question will be spoken JUST ONE TIME. They will not be written out for you. There are four parts to this test. Special instructions will be given to you at the beginning of each part.

Part A

In Part A, you will see several pictures in your test book. For each picture, you will be asked 1 to 3 questions. For each question, you will hear four possible answers. Choose the best answer according to what you see in the picture.

Example:

You will see:

You will hear: What is this?
A. This is a table.
B. This is a chair.
C. This is a watch.
D. This is a doll.

The best answer to the question "What is this?" is B: "This is a chair." Therefore, you should choose answer B.

A. <u>Questions 1-3</u>

D. <u>Questions 9-10</u>

B. <u>Questions 4-5</u>

E. <u>Questions 11-13</u>

C. <u>Questions 6-8</u>

F. <u>Questions 14-15</u>

Part B

In Part B, you will hear 15 questions. After you hear a question, read the four possible answers in your test book and decide which one is the best answer to the question you have heard.

Example:

You will hear: What does your father do?

You will read: A. He's 50 years old.
                 B. He's a teacher.
                 C. He's hungry.
                 D. He's in Los Angeles.

The best answer to the question "What does your father do?" is B: "He's a teacher." Therefore, you should choose answer B.

Please go to the next page. ⇨

16. A. Very near from here.
    B. About four hours.
    C. You can go there by train.
    D. I think you will be lost.

17. A. Yes, I don't want to go.
    B. No, I have a test in English tomorrow.
    C. Yes, I prefer to stay at home.
    D. No, I'd like to.

18. A. Their prices are reasonable for the quantity.
    B. They stopped giving money to customers.
    C. Your money isn't worth as much as before.
    D. I will sell it if the price is right.

19. A. Sure, here you are.
    B. Sure, here are you.
    C. Of course, here is it.
    D. Of course. You are here.

20. A. I'm sorry he's not home.
    B. I'm Mrs. Wang. Who are you?
    C. Where are you calling from?
    D. It's me. What's wrong?

21. A. Once a week.
    B. I like to study.
    C. I always go by bike.
    D. I leave my house at seven.

22. A. A table for two, please.
    B. Don't worry. It won't break easily.
    C. Great. I am really hungry.
    D. Can you fish?

23. A. Stand up, please.
    B. I can't go hiking with my classmate.
    C. Cheer up, Tom.
    D. It's very nice of you.

24. A. There are desks in the
       classroom.
    B. There are forty-five desks
       in it.
    C. There are many chairs in
       the classroom.
    D. There are many desks
       in it.

25. A. Sweet-and-sour pork
       tastes delicious.
    B. I've never tasted sweet-
       and-sour chicken.
    C. I also bought some
       vegetables.
    D. Meat was too expensive
       today.

26. A. It is John.
    B. It isn't me.
    C. Mary did.
    D. My younger brother does.

27. A. Yes, it is. It's hers.
    B. No, it isn't. It's mine.
    C. Yes, they are. They're
       hers.
    D. No, they aren't. They
       aren't mine.

28. A. Maybe you are right.
    B. Yes, I hate noise.
    C. Yes, it's so exciting.
    D. No, people in big cities
       are friendly.

29. A. I don't see it.
    B. It is very hard to learn.
    C. I don't know.
    D. This road is a nice road.

30. A. I am going to America.
    B. You would know that
       if you asked me.
    C. I lived here last year.
    D. I have been to California.

Part C

In Part C, you will hear 15 conversations between a man and a woman. After each conversation, you will hear a question about the conversation. After you hear the question, read the four possible answers in your test book and choose the best answer to the question you have heard.

Example:

<u>You will hear:</u> (Man) How do you go to school every day?
(Woman) Usually by bus. Sometimes by taxi.

TONE: How does the woman go to school?

<u>You will read:</u> A. She always goes to school on foot.
B. She usually takes a bike.
C. She takes either a bus or a taxi.
D. She usually goes to school by bus, never by taxi.

The best answer to the question "How does the woman go to school?" is C: "She takes either a bus or a taxi." Therefore, you should choose answer C.

Please go to the next page. ⇨

31. A. Six o'clock.
    B. Seven o'clock.
    C. Eight o'clock.
    D. Eight-thirty.

32. A. Driver.
    B. Construction worker.
    C. Mechanic.
    D. Plumber.

33. A. Vegetables.
    B. Cereal and vegetables.
    C. Cereals and bananas.
    D. Rice and mashed
       vegetables.

34. A. He publishes newspapers.
    B. He is an author.
    C. He collects automobiles.
    D. He works in industry.

35. A. He made money at first.
    B. He can't sell books.
    C. He and his boss get along
       well.
    D. He prefers to be a fireman.

36. A. Setting the table.
    B. Polishing silver.
    C. Sewing napkins.
    D. Stocking a pantry.

37. A. Her son was slapped.
    B. Her son is a troublemaker.
    C. Her son has bad grades.
    D. The teacher isn't
       competent.

38. A. In another building.
    B. In his office.
    C. In the bathroom.
    D. In a meeting.

39. A. 160 lbs.
    B. 150 lbs.
    C. 163 lbs.
    D. 153 lbs.

40. A. Mow the lawn.
    B. Weed the flowers.
    C. Pay $50 a month for a
       gardener.
    D. Work in the flower beds.

41. A. The man and woman shopped all over town.
    B. The woman went to many different stores.
    C. The woman bought some bookcases on sale.
    D. The man sold the woman some expensive bookcases.

42. A. He read the newspaper.
    B. One of his students told him.
    C. He listened to a radio report.
    D. He attended a cabinet meeting.

43. A. Herself.
    B. Mabel Anderson.
    C. The man.
    D. Marty.

44. A. His father is sick.
    B. He doesn't like school.
    C. He causes a lot of trouble.
    D. He's a poor student.

45. A. Lawyer.
    B. Detective.
    C. Policeman.
    D. Psychiatrist.

Part D

In Part D, you will hear 15 short talks.   After each talk, you will hear a question about the talk.   After you hear the question, read the four possible answers in your test book and choose the best answer to the question you have heard.

Example:

<u>You will hear:</u>   Well, that's all for Unit 15.   For today's homework, please do the review questions on page 80, and we'll check the answers tomorrow. Now, let's go on to Unit 16.

TONE: What is the teacher going to do next in today's class?

<u>You will read:</u>   A. Check the homework.
B. Review Unit 15.
C. Start a new unit.
D. Answer students' questions.

The best answer to the question "What is the teacher going to do next in today's class?" is C: "Start a new unit."   Therefore, you should choose answer C.

Please go to the next page. ⇨

46. A. Men.
    B. Aboriginal men.
    C. Women.
    D. Aboriginal women.

47. A. A gun.
    B. A knife.
    C. A bomb.
    D. A club.

48. A. Tipping in restaurants.
    B. Different kinds of
       restaurants.
    C. A good restaurant.
    D. A self-service restaurant.

49. A. 27.
    B. 16.
    C. None.
    D. The speaker does not tell.

50. A. A driver and five passengers.
    B. A driver and five pedestrians.
    C. Five pedestrians.
    D. Two drivers.

51. A. American film making.
    B. American values.
    C. Early American life.
    D. Western films.

52. A. Italian music.
    B. Western music.
    C. Western opera.
    D. Romantic opera.

53. A. A home for old Victorians.
    B. A restaurant.
    C. A home for hundreds of
       paying guests.
    D. A home for a few paying
       guests.

54. A. Buying theater tickets
       well in advance.
    B. Buying theater tickets at
       the box office.
    C. Going to the theaters in
       Taipei.
    D. Last-minute discounts on
       theater tickets.

55. A. Bonn.
    B. Munich.
    C. Vienna.
    D. London.

56. A. A bus driver.
    B. A hotel clerk.
    C. A tour guide.
    D. A traveller.

57. A. A baseball player.
    B. Stephen Yang.
    C. A couch.
    D. A sportscaster.

58. A. Arriving passengers.
    B. Departing passengers.
    C. People boarding a boat.
    D. People departing from a train.

59. A. A child.
    B. A bear.
    C. An author.
    D. A pig.

60. A. Famous athletes.
    B. Televised sports.
    C. Sports news.
    D. Reporters.

Listening Test 8 詳解

Part A

For questions number 1 to 3, please look at picture A.

1. (**C**) Question number 1, what is the young man riding?
    A. He is riding a bicycle.
    B. He is riding a horse.
    C. He is riding a motorcycle.
    D. He is riding a mule.
    * mule (mjul) *n.* 騾

2. (**D**) Question number 2, please look at picture A again. What did the young man drive through?
    A. He drove through a river.
    B. He drove through a pool.
    C. He drove through a hole.
    D. He drove through a puddle.
    * puddle ('pʌdḷ) *n.* 水坑

3. (**B**) Question number 3, please look at picture A again. Where is the old man standing?
    A. He is standing on a bench.
    B. He is standing on the sidewalk.
    C. He is standing on the wall.
    D. He is standing on the motorbike.
    * sidewalk ('saɪd,wɔk) *n.* 人行道

For questions number 4 to 5, please look at picture B.

4. (**C**) Question number 4, where are the children?
    A. They are at a zoo.
    B. They are at school.
    C. They are at a park.
    D. They are at home.

5. (**B**) Question number 5, please look at picture B again. What is the girl on the left doing?
  A. She is holding a ball.
  B. She is swinging.
  C. She is talking with the boy.
  D. She is running.

  * swing〔swɪŋ〕v. 搖擺；盪鞦韆

For questions number 6 to 8, please look at picture C.

6. (**B**) Question number 6, what is the man doing?
  A. He is talking to the woman.
  B. He is mugging the woman.
  C. He is taking a walk with the woman.
  D. He is trying to marry the woman.

  * mug〔mʌg〕v. 搶劫

7. (**C**) Question number 7, please look at picture C again. How does the woman feel?
  A. She feels delighted.
  B. She feels depressed.
  C. She feels frightened.
  D. She feels comfortable.

  * delighted〔dɪ'laɪtɪd〕adj. 高興的   depressed〔dɪ'prɛst〕adj. 沮喪的

8. (**B**) Question number 8, please look at picture C again. What does the man have?
  A. He has a knife.
  B. He has a gun.
  C. He has a bomb.
  D. He has a stick.

  * bomb〔bɑm〕n. 炸彈   stick〔stɪk〕n. 棍子

For questions number 9 to 10, please look at picture D.

9. (**A**) Question number 9, what is the man on the right doing?

      A. He is hailing a taxi.

      B. He is saying goodbye to the taxi.

      C. He is paying the taxi driver.

      D. He is driving a taxi.

      * hail (hel) *v.* 招呼

10. (**C**) Question number 10, please look at picture D again.　How is the traffic?

      A. It is heavy.

      B. It is fast.

      C. It is light.

      D. It is slow.

For questions number 11 to 13, please look at picture E.

11. (**D**) Question number 11, how is the music?

      A. The music is soft.

      B. The music is hard.

      C. The music is broken.

      D. The music is loud.

12. (**B**) Question number 12, please look at picture E again.　What is the man on the left doing?

      A. He is drinking.

      B. He is smoking a cigarette.

      C. He is doing the dishes.

      D. He is cooking.

      * *do the dishes* 洗碗盤

13. (**D**) Question number 13, please look at picture E again.　What is on the floor?
　　A. A clock.
　　B. A calendar.
　　C. A woman.
　　D. A cat.

For questions number 14 to 15, please look at picture F.

14. (**C**) Question number 14, what is the boy wearing?
　　A. He is wearing a uniform.
　　B. He is wearing a swimsuit.
　　C. He is wearing pajamas.
　　D. He is wearing shorts.

　　 * pajamas (pə'dʒæməs) *n.* 睡衣褲　　shorts (ʃɔrts) *n.* 短褲

15. (**A**) Question number 15, please look at picture F again.　What is the woman doing?
　　A. She is serving coffee.
　　B. She is reading newspapers.
　　C. She is pouring tea.
　　D. She is making breakfast.

Part B

16. (**B**) How long is it to Taipei?
　　A. Very near from here.
　　B. About four hours.
　　C. You can go there by train.
　　D. I think you will be lost.

17. (**B**) Don't you want to go to the movies?
　　A. Yes, I don't want to go.
　　B. No, I have a test in English tomorrow.
　　C. Yes, I prefer to stay at home.
　　D. No, I'd like to.

18. (**A**)　Does that restaurant give you your money's worth?

       A. Their prices are reasonable for the quantity.

       B. They stopped giving money to customers.

       C. Your money isn't worth as much as before.

       D. I will sell it if the price is right.

19. (**A**)　Could you pass the dictionary, please?

       A. Sure, here you are.

       B. Sure, here are you.

       C. Of course, here is it.

       D. Of course.　You are here.

       * pass (pæs) *v.* 傳遞

20. (**A**)　Hello.　May I speak to Mr. Wang, please?

       A. I'm sorry he's not home.

       B. I'm Mrs. Wang. Who are you?

       C. Where are you calling from?

       D. It's me.　What's wrong?

21. (**C**)　How do you go to class?

       A. Once a week.

       B. I like to study.

       C. I always go by bike.

       D. I leave my house at seven.

22. (**C**)　Shall we break for lunch?

       A. A table for two, please.

       B. Don't worry.　It won't break easily.

       C. Great.　I am really hungry.

       D. Can you fish?

       * break (brek) *v.* 休息

23. (**B**) Why do you look so down?
  A. Stand up, please.
  B. I can't go hiking with my classmate.
  C. Cheer up, Tom.
  D. It's very nice of you.

  * down (daʊn) *adj.* 沮喪的　　***cheer up*** 振作起來

24. (**B**) How many desks are there in the classroom?
  A. There are desks in the classroom.
  B. There are forty-five desks in it.
  C. There are many chairs in the classroom.
  D. There are many desks in it.

25. (**D**) Why didn't you buy beef and pork?
  A. Sweet-and-sour pork tastes delicious.
  B. I've never tasted sweet-and-sour chicken.
  C. I also bought some vegetables.
  D. Meat was too expensive today.

  * sweet-and-sour ('switən,saʊr) *adj.* 糖醋的
  pork (pork) *n.* 豬肉

26. (**C**) Who broke the window?
  A. It is John.
  B. It isn't me.
  C. Mary did.
  D. My younger brother does.

27. (**C**) Are these Mary's clothes?
  A. Yes, it is.　It's hers.
  B. No, it isn't.　It's mine.
  C. Yes, they are.　They're hers.
  D. No, they aren't.　They aren't mine.

28. (**C**) Do you like life in a big city?
    A. Maybe you are right.
    B. Yes, I hate noise.
    C. Yes, it's so exciting.
    D. No, people in big cities are friendly.

29. (**C**) Where does this road go?
    A. I don't see it.
    B. It is very hard to learn.
    C. I don't know.
    D. This road is a nice road.

30. (**D**) I haven't seen you for a long time.
    A. I am going to America.
    B. You would know that if you asked me.
    C. I lived here last year.
    D. I have been to California.

Part C

31. (**D**) M: Hurry up! It's already eight o'clock and the Harrisons will be arriving any second now.
    W: Oh, I forgot to tell you. Mr. Harrison called at seven to say they'd be half an hour late. He didn't get off work until six.

    (TONE)
    Q: When will the Harrisons arrive?
    A. Six o'clock.
    B. Seven o'clock.
    C. Eight o'clock.
    D. Eight-thirty.

    * *any second* 隨時 (= *any moment*)   *get off* 結束 (工作)

32. (**C**) M: That will be fifty dollars for the tune-up and oil change.
　　　　　　 I also checked your brakes.
　　　　　 W: Did you find out what was causing that rattle in the trunk?

　　　 (TONE)
　　　 Q: What is the man's occupation?
　　　 A. Driver.
　　　 B. Construction worker.
　　　 C. Mechanic.
　　　 D. Plumber.

　　　 * tune-up ('tjun,ʌp) *n.* 調整 (使進入最佳狀況)　　*oil change* 換潤滑油
　　　　 brake (brek) *n.* 煞車　　 rattle ('rætl) *n.* 格格聲
　　　　 trunk (trʌŋk) *n.* 行李箱　　*construction worker* 建築工人
　　　　 mechanic (mə'kænɪk) *n.* 技工　　 plumber ('plʌmɚ) *n.* 水管工人

33. (**C**) M: Is your baby on solid food yet?　Ours isn't.
　　　　　 W: Oh, yes.　He's had rice cereals and mashed bananas so far,
　　　　　　　 and I'm going to try him on vegetables next week.

　　　 (TONE)
　　　 Q: What does the baby eat now?
　　　 A. Vegetables.
　　　 B. Cereal and vegetables.
　　　 C. Cereals and bananas.
　　　 D. Rice and mashed vegetables.

　　　 * solid ('salɪd) *adj.* 固體的　　 cereal ('sɪrɪəl) *n.* 穀類食品
　　　　 mashed (mæʃt) *adj.* 搗成泥的

34. (**B**) W: Paul is so busy lately, I never have a chance to talk to him
　　　　　　　 anymore.　How's he doing?
　　　　　 M: He had a collection of verse published last year, and now
　　　　　　　 he's trying to get a novel about the automobile industry.

(TONE)

Q: What does Paul do?

A. He publishes newspapers.

B. He is an author.

C. He collects automobiles.

D. He works in industry.

* **collection of verse** 詩集　　author (ˈɔθɚ) n. 作家

35. (**B**) W: How's your new job with the book company?

M: It seemed promising at first, but I guess I'm no salesman. And to add fuel to the fire, the boss and I have our differences.

(TONE)

Q: What do we know about the man's job?

A. He made money at first.

B. He can't sell books.

C. He and his boss get along well.

D. He prefers to be a fireman.

* promising (ˈprɑmɪsɪŋ) adj. 大有可爲的
  add fuel to the fire 火上加油　　**get along well** 相處愉快

36. (**A**) W: Does everything look all right to you? I want it to be perfect.

M: I think you've made a mistake. Don't the napkins go on the left and the silverware on the right?

(TONE)

Q: What are the two people discussing?

A. Setting the table.　　B. Polishing silver.

C. Sewing napkins.　　D. Stocking a pantry.

* napkin (ˈnæpkɪn) n. 餐巾　　silverware (ˈsɪlvɚ͵wɛr) n. 銀餐具
  set the table 擺好餐具　　polish (ˈpɑlɪʃ) v. 擦亮
  sew (so) v. 縫製　　stock (stɑk) v. 儲貨
  pantry (ˈpæntrɪ) n. 食品儲藏室

37. (**A**) W: If you ever slap my poor little child again, I'll complain to the school board!

    M: You'll find no sympathy on the school board. Your son is the most notorious troublemaker that ever passed through the doors of this high school.

(TONE)

Q: Why is the woman angry?

A. Her son was slapped.

B. Her son is a troublemaker.

C. Her son has bad grades.

D. The teacher isn't competent.

* slap (slæp) v. 打~耳光   board (bord) n. 董事會
troublemaker ('trʌbl̩ˌmekɚ) n. 惹麻煩的人
competent ('kɑmpətənt) adj. 有能力勝任的

38. (**D**) M: If I were you I wouldn't interrupt the boss while he's in an important meeting. Wait until he comes back to his office.

    W: If I were you I'd mind my own business. He told me to bring him this information as soon as it arrived, even if he was in the bathroom.

(TONE)

Q: Where is the boss?

A. In another building.   B. In his office.

C. In the bathroom.   D. In a meeting.

* interrupt (ˌɪntəˈrʌpt) v. 打斷
mind one's own business 管好自己的事；別多管閒事
as soon as 一~（就）

39. (**D**) M: Susan told me you were on a diet. How much weight have you lost?

    W: Well, to start with, I weighed 160 pounds. The first two weeks I took off 10 pounds, but then I gained back 3 over the holidays.

(TONE)

Q: How much does the woman weigh now?

A. 160 lbs.   B. 150 lbs.

C. 163 lbs.   D. 153 lbs.

* *on a diet* 節食   weigh〔we〕*v.* 有～的重量

   lbs. 磅（= *pounds*）

40. (**D**) M: Your yard is always so beautiful, Cathy. You must have a gardener.

W: Oh, no. It would cost at least $50 a month to hire someone to do the work, so I do most of it myself. I enjoy taking care of the flowers, but I have to force myself to do the weeding and cut the grass.

(TONE)

Q: What does Cathy like to do?

A. Mow the lawn.

B. Weed the flowers.

C. Pay $50 a month for a gardener.

D. Work in the flower beds.

* yard〔jɑrd〕*n.* 庭院   *do the weeding* 除雜草   mow〔mo〕*v.* 割

41. (**B**) M: Did you find what you wanted? You've been gone all afternoon.

W: I looked all over town, but couldn't find any bookcases on sale. They're so expensive. I guess I'll wait a while longer.

(TONE)

Q: What is obvious from the conversation?

A. The man and woman shopped all over town.

B. The woman went to many different stores.

C. The woman bought some bookcases on sale.

D. The man sold the woman some expensive bookcases.

* bookcase〔'buk,kes〕*n.* 書櫃   *on sale* 拍賣中

42. (**A**) W: Professor Horton, have you heard the morning news
　　　　 report?　Smith resigned his post as defense secretary.

　　　 M: I didn't turn on the radio this morning, but I did see the
　　　　 headlines.　If you remember, he threatened to leave office
　　　　 at the last cabinet meeting.

　　　 (TONE)

　　　 Q: How did the professor learn that the defense secretary had
　　　　 resigned?

　　　 A. He read the newspaper.
　　　 B. One of his students told him.
　　　 C. He listened to a radio report.
　　　 D. He attended a cabinet meeting.

　　　 * *defense secretary* 國防部長　　*turn on* 打開
　　　　 headline ('hɛd,laɪn) *n.* 標題　　cabinet ('kæbənɪt) *n.* 內閣

43. (**C**) M: Mabel Anderson makes me furious.　She can't keep a
　　　　 secret.　I told her about our engagement and she said she
　　　　 wouldn't tell anyone.　But two hours later, everyone was
　　　　 talking about our upcoming marriage.　Even Marty and
　　　　 Roger know about it.

　　　 W: You're the one who can't keep a secret.

　　　 (TONE)

　　　 Q: Whom does the woman blame for revealing the secret?

　　　 A. Herself.
　　　 B. Mabel Anderson.
　　　 C. The man.
　　　 D. Marty.

　　　 * furious ('fjʊrɪəs) *adj.* 狂怒的
　　　　 upcoming ('ʌp,kʌmɪŋ) *adj.* 即將來臨的
　　　　 reveal (rɪ'vil) *v.* 洩露

44. (**D**) W: What angers me is not your poor grades, but the fact that you hardly tried.　We have no choice other than expelling you.

M: But you aren't even considering my personal problems.　How am I supposed to concentrate on books when my father is in the hospital with cancer?

(TONE)

Q: Why is the boy being expelled?

A. His father is sick.

B. He doesn't like school.

C. He causes a lot of trouble.

D. He's a poor student.

* expel (ɪk'spɛl) v. 開除　concentrate ('kɑnsɛn,tret) v. 全神貫注
  cancer ('kænsə) n. 癌症

45. (**B**) W: I suspect that my husband is having an affair with another woman.　However, my lawyer tells me I need proof before I can sue my husband for divorce.　It is my hope, therefore, that you can turn up some proof which I can use in court.

M: Well, Mrs. Blaine, if he's cheating on you we will get the evidence.　We charge ten dollars an hour and we'll need a deposit of one hundred dollars.

(TONE)

Q: What is the man's occupation?

A. Lawyer.

B. Detective.

C. Policeman.

D. Psychiatrist.

* suspect (sə'spɛkt) v. 懷疑　affair (ə'fɛr) n. 戀情
  turn up 找到　charge (tʃɑrdʒ) v. 收費
  deposit (dɪ'pɑzɪt) n. 保證金　detective (dɪ'tɛktɪv) n. 偵探
  psychiatrist (saɪ'kaɪətrɪst) n. 精神病學家

Part D

46. (**B**) An estimated two million Taiwan residents, or 17 percent of all men and one percent of all women, chew betel nut regularly.　Among the aboriginal population, the ratio increases to 46.5 percent of men and 38 percent of women.

(TONE)

Q: Who chew the most betel nut?

A. Men.

B. Aboriginal men.

C. Women.

D. Aboriginal women.

* estimated (ˈɛstə͵metɪd) *adj.* 據估計的　　resident (ˈrɛzədənt) *n.* 居民
chew (tʃu) *v.* 嚼　　*betel nut* 檳榔
aboriginal (͵æbəˈrɪdʒənl) *adj.* 原住民的　　ratio (ˈreʃo) *n.* 比率

47. (**D**) An elderly man was mugged as he walked through Youth Park yesterday afternoon.　He was hit several times on the head with a blunt instrument.　The attacker fled before the police arrived.

(TONE)

Q: What did the attacker probably use as a weapon?

A. A gun.　　　　　B. A knife.

C. A bomb.　　　　D. A club.

* mug (mʌg) *v.* 搶劫　　blunt (blʌnt) *adj.* 鈍的
flee (fli) *v.* 逃走 (過去式 fled)　　club (klʌb) *n.* 棍棒

48. (**D**) If you are in a hurry and you want to have a quick meal, there is no better place than a self-service restaurant.　You pick out what you want and put it on your tray, which you have to push along a special rack till you reach the cashier.　The cashier will give you your bill.　You can sit alone or with another customer. And as there is no waiter, you don't have to give a tip.

(TONE)

Q: What is this talk about?

A. Tipping in restaurants.

B. Different kinds of restaurants.

C. A good restaurant.

D. A self-service restaurant.

* *pick out* 挑出   tray〔tre〕*n.* 托盤
  rack〔ræk〕*n.* 架子   cashier〔kæ'ʃɪr〕*n.* 收銀員
  bill〔bɪl〕*n.* 帳單   tip〔tɪp〕*n.* 小費

49. (**D**) An earthquake shook the city and the surrounding area at 2:07 a.m. today. The earthquake was the area's strongest since the 1988 quake, which claimed 16 lives.

(TONE)

Q: How many people died in today's earthquake?

A. 27.

B. 16.

C. None.

D. The speaker does not tell.

* claim〔klem〕*v.* (事故) 奪走 (生命)

50. (**C**) Five pedestrians were seriously injured when a truck's brakes failed yesterday. The driver escaped unhurt. The pedestrians were rushed to a hospital and treated for shock.

(TONE)

Q: Who were injured?

A. A driver and five passengers.

B. A driver and five pedestrians.

C. Five pedestrians.

D. Two drivers.

* pedestrian〔pə'dɛstrɪən〕*n.* 行人   injure〔'ɪndʒə〕*v.* 傷害
  brake〔brek〕*n.* 煞車

51. (**D**) Western films are based on legendary early American life in the Mid-West.　Such films are very popular in the United States.　Perhaps this film genre, more than any other, can show the basis for American values and attitudes.

(TONE)

Q: What is the topic of this talk?

A. American film making.

B. American values.

C. Early American life.

D. Western films.

　* legendary ('lɛdʒəndˌɛrɪ) *adj.* 傳說的　　genre ('ʒɑnrə) *n.* 類型

52. (**C**) Western opera was developed in Europe, and many operas are Italian.　Older people rather than younger people appreciate the opera.　Costumes and stage properties are usually quite lavish and traditional to match the themes of the music which are often highly romantic.

(TONE)

Q: What is the topic of this talk?

A. Italian music.

B. Western music.

C. Western opera.

D. Romantic opera.

　* costume ('kɑstjum) *n.* 戲裝　　properties ('prɑpətɪz) *n.* 道具
　　lavish ('lævɪʃ) *adj.* 豐富的　　themes (θim) *n.* 主題

53. (**D**) A boarding house is a private home that takes in paying guests and provides meals and lodging.　In a large old Victorian house, there might be as many as 7 or 8 lodgers.

(TONE)

Q: What is a boarding house?

A. A home for old Victorians.
B. A restaurant.
C. A home for hundreds of paying guests.
D. A home for a few paying guests.

* ***boarding house*** 供膳寄宿舍   lodging (ˈlɑdʒɪŋ) *n.* 寄宿
Victorian (vɪkˈtorɪən) *adj.* 維多利亞式的
lodger (ˈlɑdʒɚ) *n.* 房客

54. (**A**) If you want to be certain of seeing a play in Taipei, you have
to book your seat in advance.   You can buy your tickets either
at a theater ticket agency or at the box office in the theater
itself.   It is very rarely that you will be lucky enough to get
a ticket five minutes before the play begins.

(TONE)

Q: What does the speaker recommend?

A. Buying theater tickets well in advance.
B. Buying theater tickets at the box office.
C. Going to the theaters in Taipei.
D. Last-minute discounts on theater tickets.

* book (buk) *v.* 預訂   ***in advance*** 事先
agency (ˈedʒənsɪ) *n.* 經銷處   ***box office*** 售票處
rarely (ˈrɛrlɪ) *adv.* 罕見地   ***last-minute discount*** 最後折扣

55. (**C**) Beethoven is universally recognized as one of the greatest
composers in the world.   Born in Bonn in 1770, Beethoven
showed great talent at an early age.   In 1787, Beethoven first
visited Vienna, at that time the center of the musical world.
There he performed before Mozart, who was amazed at his
talent.

(TONE)

Q: Where did Mozart see Beethoven perform?

A. Bonn.   B. Munich.

C. Vienna.   D. London.

* composer (kəm'pozɚ) *n.* 作曲家   Bonn (bɑn) *n.* 波昂
amazed (ə'mezd) *adj.* 吃驚的   Munich ('mjunɪk) *n.* 慕尼黑
Vienna (vɪ'ɛnə) *n.* 維也納

56. (**C**) We will be arriving in a few minutes, so I'd like to explain a
few things. First, take all items you've stowed overhead or at
your seat with you. Next, you'll find a table in the lobby
where we'll check in. Just tell the clerk your name and pick
up your room key.

(TONE)

Q: Who is making this announcement?

A. A bus driver.   B. A hotel clerk.

C. A tour guide.   D. A traveller.

* item ('aɪtəm) *n.* 物件   stow (sto) *v.* 堆置
overhead ('ovɚ'hɛd) *adv.* 在上面   lobby ('lɑbɪ) *n.* 大廳
check in 登記住宿   clerk (klɜk) *n.* 辦事員   ***tour guide*** 導遊

57. (**D**) Lions one, Elephants nothing. Three and two. Two out.
Mike Row checks the runner and throws. Stephen Yang's
trying to hit a winning run. He swings. It's strike three.

(TONE)

Q: Who is speaking?

A. A baseball player.

B. Stephen Yang.

C. A coach.

D. A sportscaster.

* check (tʃɛk) *v.* 檢查   run (rʌn) *n.* 跑壘   swing (swɪŋ) *v.* 揮棒
strike (straɪk) *n.* 好球   coach (kotʃ) *n.* 教練
sportscaster ('sports,kæstɚ) *n.* 比賽實況轉播廣播員

58. (**A**) Let me be the first to welcome you to Middletown. I hope you've had a pleasant journey. If you are connecting to another flight, an attendant at the gate will give you the departure gate number for your next flight.

(TONE)

Q: To whom is this announcement most likely directed?

A. Arriving passengers.
B. Departing passengers.
C. People boarding a boat.
D. People departing from a train.

* attendant (ə'tɛndənt) *n.* 服務人員　　gate (get) *n.* 出入口
　departure gate 離境登機門

59. (**C**) I always like to begin the first day of class with some English literature that is less serious and somewhat playful. *Winnie-the-Pooh*. This is a book of tales about a happy little bear named Pooh and his friends. It was written by A. A. Milne in the finest of story-telling traditions.

(TONE)

Q: Who is Milne?

A. A child.　　　　　　　B. A bear.
C. An author.　　　　　　D. A pig.

* playful ('plefəl) *adj.* 玩笑式的

60. (**C**) Sports news is very popular among many readers of newspapers and magazines. Reporters often push for interviews with athletes and players after a match, particularly with the famous ones.

(TONE)

Q: What is the speaker discussing?

A. Famous athletes.　　　　B. Televised sports.
C. Sports news.　　　　　　D. Reporters.

* *push for* 極力爭取　　athlete ('æθlit) *n.* 運動員
　match (mætʃ) *n.* 比賽　　televised ('tɛlə‚vaɪzd) *adj.* 由電視播映的

心得筆記欄

全國最完整的文法書 ☆☆☆
文法寶典
▶ 劉 毅 編著

　　這是一套想學好英文的人必備的工具書，作者積多年豐富的教學經驗，針對大家所不了解和最容易犯錯的地方，編寫成一套完整的文法書。

　　本書編排方式與眾不同，首先給讀者整體的概念，再詳述文法中的細節部分，內容十分完整。文法說明以圖表爲中心，一目了然，並且務求深入淺出。無論您在考試中或其他書中所遇到的任何不了解的問題，或是您感到最煩惱的文法問題，查閱**文法寶典**均可迎刃而解。例如：哪些副詞可修飾名詞或代名詞？(P.228)；什麼是介副詞？(P.543)；那些名詞可以當副詞用？(P.100)；倒裝句(P.629)、省略句(P.644)等特殊構句，爲什麼倒裝？爲什麼省略？原來的句子是什麼樣子？在**文法寶典**裏都有詳盡的說明。

　　例如，有人學了**觀念錯誤的**「假設法現在式」的公式，

If + 現在式動詞……，主詞 + shall (will, may, can) + 原形動詞

只會造：If it rains, I will stay at home.
而不敢造：If you *are* right, I *am* wrong.
　　　　　If I *said* that, I *was* mistaken.
　　　　　（If 子句不一定用在假設法，也可表示條件子句的直說法。）

可見如果學文法不求徹底了解，反而成爲學習英文的絆腳石，對於這些易出錯的地方，我們都特別加以說明（詳見 P.356）。

　　文法寶典每冊均附有練習，只要讀完本書、做完練習，您必定信心十足，大幅提高對英文的興趣與實力。

◉ 全套五冊，售價**900**元。市面不售，請直接向本公司購買。

中級英語檢定模考班

　　全民英語能力分級檢定測驗，任何人都可以參加，無論你的年齡，無論你的學歷，即使你現在只是國中生，如果你認爲你的程度已達到高中程度，你也可以參加，這是證明你實力最好的方法。沒有通過「中級英語檢定測驗」，未來有可能無法取得高中畢業證書。

- **開課目的：**　協助同學通過教育部所舉行的「**中級英語檢定測驗**」。
  每年舉辦兩次，同學可及早準備。

- **招生對象：**　任何人均可參加，現在的高一同學，聯考將取消，以此考試成績取代，愈早通過此項測驗愈好。

- **上課時間：**　每週一晚上 6：00～9：20（共六週）

- **上課地點：**　台北市重慶南路一段 10 號 7 F

- **上課內容：**　完全比照財團法人語言訓練中心所做「中級英語檢定測驗」初試標準。舉行 70 分鐘的模考，包含 45 題聽力測驗，及詞彙結構、克漏字、閱讀測驗共 40 題。考完試後立刻講解。

- **收費標準：**　**3800** 元（報名後即贈「中級英語聽力測驗①」書加卡帶一套，市價 1140 元，「中級英語字彙 500 題」，市價 180 元。）

- **課前預習：**　報名後利用本班發的資料，在家自行預習。

劉 毅 升大學英文家教班

台北市重慶南路一段 10 號 7 F（寶島銀行樓上）　☎（02）2381-3148・2331-8822

劉毅英文家教班高二、高三班簡章

- **招生對象：** 高二、高三同學

- **上課日期：** 全年無休

- **開課班級：**（為保障教學品質，額滿不收。）

A班	週四晚上 6：00 ～ 9：30	G班	週日下午 1：20 ～ 5：00
B班	週五晚上 6：00 ～ 9：30	I班	週二晚上 6：00 ～ 9：30
C班	週六上午 8：20 ～12：00	J班	週三晚上 6：00 ～ 9：30
D班	週六下午 1：20 ～ 5：00	N班	週五晚上 6：00 ～ 9：30
E班	週六晚上 6：00 ～ 9：30	O班	週六上午 8：20 ～12：00
F班	週日上午 8：20 ～12：00	P班	週六下午 1：20 ～ 5：00

- **教學目標：**

　　大學入學考試和以往不同，同學考了「學科能力測驗」，到了 7 月份，又要考「大學入學指定科目考試」，歷屆學科能力測驗已經考了 11 年了，題目比聯考簡單，此項考試只是跨過門檻的考試，而 7 月份的「指定科目考試」是要鑑別考生前面 60 %～ 70 % 的能力，所以試題比大學聯考稍難，根據命題原則，單作文一項就要求達到 120～150 字，單字出題範圍在教育部所規定的常用七千個字彙內。面臨此一變換，我們有完全的準備，應付今年「指定科目考試」的七種題型命題，同學只要每週準時來上課，英文這一科交給「劉毅英文」，我們用簡單的方法，考試、背書、舉行各種比賽。無論如何，到了大考時，你的英文成績就會遠遠超過其他同學。

- **獎學金制度：**

　　1. 凡報名後，過去在學校高二上下學期，或高三上學期，在班上總成績，只要有一次前三名，就可申請一次獎學金，第一名 3000 元，第二名 1000 元，第三名 1000 元。（每人限領一次。）

　　2. 高三同學上學期學校模擬考，只要有任何一次，英文成績在班上第一名的同學，就可得獎學金 3000 元。（1、2 項限領一次。）

　　3. 本班學期總成績，第一名 10000 元，第二名 9000 元，第三名 8000 元，第四名 7000 元，第五名 5000 元，以下略。

　　4. 指定科目考試成績全國英文最高分，可得獎學金壹拾萬元；96 分以上，獎學金 20000 元；90 分以上，獎學金 10000 元；80 分以上 1000 元；60 分以上者，均有獎勵。（只限高三下學期補習同學。）

學習補習班·劉毅英文（國一、國二、國三、高一、高二、高三班）

國中部：台北市重慶南路一段 10 號 7 F（消防隊斜對面）　☎ (02) 2381-3148

高中部：台北市許昌街 17 號 6 F（壽德大樓）　☎ (02) 2389-5212

劉毅專爲高中同學設計的新資料

教科書版本各校不同，但是，同學都要參加「大學入學學科能力測驗」，也要參加「全民英語能力分級檢定」。學習出版公司負責人劉毅老師，特別準備好了一套完整的教材，協助高中同學輕鬆通過考試，達到目標。學生用書只有題目，沒有解答，適合老師教學使用。

1. 中級英語文法測驗 （25K，共203頁，售價180元，學生用書16K，100頁，售價120元）

這是最新發明學文法的方法，只要做完練習題，文法就通了。全書共有50回測驗，每回測驗10題。每條題目的解答，都有中文翻譯及詳細的文法分析，對錯答案都有明確的交代。

2. 中級英語字彙500題 （25K，共208頁，售價180元，學生用書16K，107頁，售價120元）

全書分爲50回測驗，每回測驗10題，從大規模考試中，**電腦統計出最常考的字彙**，題目型式與學科能力測驗、指定科目考試相同。**特殊編排，同學一看就會有想做的衝動**，每條題目都有中文翻譯，每個單字都有音標及註解。

3. 中級英語克漏字測驗 （25K，共219頁，售價180元，學生用書16K，70頁，售價100元）

本書共有50回克漏字測驗，每篇文章均有中文翻譯，及詳細的文法分析，每條題目的答案，都有明確交代，對與錯均有說明。

4. 中級英語閱讀測驗 （25K，共235頁，售價180元，學生用書16K，100頁，售價120元）

全書有50篇閱讀測驗，每篇文章均有中文翻譯及詳細的文法分析，生字均有註解，閱讀此書完全不需要查字典，書中並附有**閱讀測驗答題技巧**。

5. 中級英語聽力檢定① 中級英語聽力檢定② （本套書共分二冊，25K，每冊240頁，書售價180元，學生用書16K，70頁，售價120元，各附卡帶8捲960元）

專爲高中同學準備「全民英語能力檢定」聽力測驗而設計，本套書也適用於「大學入學推薦甄試第二階段的聽力測驗」。**訓練聽力愈早愈好**。

6. 中級英語寫作口說測驗 （25K，共160頁，書售價180元，卡帶4捲500元）

本書針對「中級英語檢定測驗第二階段複試測驗」而編寫，書中包含**中譯英、英文作文、朗讀短文、回答問題**，及**看圖敘述**。本書全部經過劉毅英文「**中級英語檢定複試班**」，實際在課堂上使用過，該班同學參加中級英語檢定複試測驗後，都高分通過，同學都認爲，**這套試題和實際考試非常接近**。

Editorial Staff

● **主編** / 劉　毅

● **編輯** / 謝靜芳・蔡琇瑩・高瑋謙

● **校閱** / Laura E. Stewart

● **封面設計** / 張國光

● **打字** / 黃淑貞・蘇淑玲

|||||||||||||||| ●學習出版公司門市部●||||||||||||||||||

台北地區：台北市許昌街 10 號 2 樓 TEL：(02)2331-4060・2331-9209
台中地區：台中市綠川東街 32 號 8 樓 23 室
TEL：(04)2223-2838

|||||||||||||||||||||||||||||||||||||||||||||||||||||||

中級英語聽力檢定①

主　　　編／劉　毅
發　行　所／學習出版有限公司　　　☎ (02) 2704-5525
郵　撥　帳　號／0512727-2 學習出版社帳戶
登　記　證／局版台業 2179 號
印　刷　所／裕強彩色印刷有限公司
台 北 門 市／台北市許昌街 10 號 2 F　　☎ (02) 2331-4060・2331-9209
台 中 門 市／台中市綠川東街 32 號 8 F 23 室　　☎ (04) 2223-2838
台灣總經銷／紅螞蟻圖書有限公司　　☎ (02) 2795-3656
美國總經銷／ Evergreen Book Store　　☎ (818) 2813622
本公司網址　www.learnbook.com.tw
電子郵件　learnbook@learnbook.com.tw

售價：新台幣一百八十元正

2004 年 6 月 1 日一版五刷

ISBN 957-519-526-6